# Apple-achian Treasure

# Also by this Author

**Mystery/Suspense:**

*Auntie Clem's Bakery*
Gluten-Free Murder
Dairy-Free Death
Allergen-Free Assignation
Witch-Free Halloween (Halloween Short)
Dog-Free Dinner (Christmas Short)
Stirring Up Murder
Brewing Death
Coup de Glace
Sour Cherry Turnover
Apple-achian Treasure
Vegan Baked Alaska (Coming Soon)

*Reg Rawlins, Psychic Detective*
What the Cat Knew
A Psychic with Catitude
A Catastrophic Theft

*Zachary Goldman Mysteries*
She Wore Mourning
His Hands Were Quiet
She Was Dying Anyway
He Was Walking Alone
They Thought He was Safe (Coming Soon)
He was Not There (Coming Soon)
Her Work was Everything (Coming Soon)

*Kenzie Kirsch Medical Thrillers*
Unlawful Harvest (Coming Soon)

Cowritten with D. D. VanDyke
*California Corwin P. I. Mystery Series*
The Girl in the Morgue

*Stand Alone Suspense Novels*
Looking Over Your Shoulder
Lion Within
Pursued by the Past
In the Tick of Time
Loose the Dogs

## Young Adult Fiction:

*Tamara's Teardrops:*
Tattooed Teardrops
Two Teardrops
Tortured Teardrops
Vanishing Teardrops

*Between the Cracks:*
Ruby
June and Justin
Michelle
Chloe
Ronnie
June, Into the Light (Coming Soon)

## And more at pdworkman.com

# Apple-achian Treasure

### Auntie Clem's Bakery #8

### P.D. Workman

pd workman

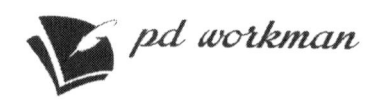

Copyright © 2019 P.D. Workman

All rights reserved. No part of this publication may be reproduced, stored in retrieval system, copied in any form or by any means, electronic, mechanical, photocopying, recording or otherwise transmitted without written permission from the publisher. You must not circulate this book in any format.

ISBN: 9781989080771

*To all who search for the true treasure in family and friends.*

## Chapter One

ERIN FIT HER KEY in the lock and found herself holding her breath as she turned it. The lock clicked smoothly open and Erin pushed the door open. She turned to look back over her shoulder at Vic as she entered.

"It feels pretty weird," she said.

Vic nodded. "I know. But it's just a different location. It's still Auntie Clem's Bakery."

Erin took a deep breath in and let it out again. "Yeah… just the same."

But it didn't feel the same. She knew she should be ecstatic about being able to open the bakery again. If not for her half-sister, Charley, allowing her to become half-owner in The Bake Shoppe and to reopen it as Auntie Clem's Bakery, that would have been the end of Erin's dream. She would have had to liquidate everything and to figure out how she was going to make a living without the bakery.

Charley's offer had seemed like a godsend at the time, but Erin had become increasingly worried about how it was all going to work out. She barely knew Charley. They hadn't grown up together and their personalities were diametrically opposed. It seemed like everything Charley did rubbed Erin the wrong way, even when she wasn't really doing anything wrong.

And now they were connected not only by blood, but in the business. They had to agree on advertising campaigns, product lines, prices, and promotions. They had to agree on everything that Erin had previously set up, like the ladies' tea after Sunday services, catering for the book club at The Book Nook across the street, and the children's cookie club.

Even just stocking the kitchen had been an ordeal, since Charley wanted to use all of the equipment that had remained from The Bake Shoppe and Erin couldn't use gluten-contaminated bowls and baking sheets to make her gluten-free baking. While Charley had agreed to continue to keep Auntie Clem's Bakery gluten-free, she didn't have the understanding Erin did and thought that they could cut a few corners. Erin wasn't willing to put the health and lives of her allergic or intolerant customers at risk.

Erin turned on the lights and looked around the kitchen. It was her bakery. It was the new normal. She and Vic could continue to work together, just as they had in the shop that had burned down. It would be almost the same.

Almost, but not quite.

Vic strode into the kitchen, where she pulled a clean apron off the hook and tied it around her slim form, then put on a hat, making sure that her long blond hair was all properly tucked away. Normal, routine actions, just like she had followed every day at the old Auntie Clem's. Erin followed suit. She was considerably shorter than Vic and her hair was shorter and dark. She felt a little better once suited up. Her uniform helped to set the mood.

She went to the fridge and started pulling out the batters they had made the night before, working through her mental checklists to get everything started in the right order so that they would have the case filled efficiently by the time the bakery opened in a few hours.

"Do we have chocolate chip muffins today?" Vic questioned.

"Yes. And blueberry. And the rice bran. I'm going to work a high-protein muffin into the lineup once we've had a chance to settle back into the schedule. Not today, but maybe next week. I'm hoping we can tap into the low-carb and paleo markets."

Vic nodded, already aware that Erin had been working on it. "You're finding some low-carb recipes that don't rely on nut flours?"

They worked side by side, finding their rhythm even in the less familiar kitchen.

"I'm focusing on some of the less allergenic seeds like *sacha inchi*. It's one of the new flours out there and becoming more available. We can grind it here so that we know that they haven't been processed on the same equipment as peanuts or tree nuts."

"You're always on top of all of the new developments."

"Well, that's my job."

Vic glanced at the clock on the wall. "I thought Charley said she was going to come in this morning to help out."

Erin didn't look at Vic and tried to keep her expression neutral. "That's what she said."

"But you didn't expect her to get here, did you?"

"Uh… no. She's really not a morning person, and this is early even for morning people. Maybe if Charley came in and helped out now, and then went home and went to bed…"

Vic chuckled. "She's like a teenager. If she wants to be a business owner, she's going to have to make a few changes to her lifestyle."

Erin turned on one of the mixers, then went around to the ovens, setting the preheat temperatures. It was the coolest part of the day, but that was about to end. Once they had the ovens going, even the best air conditioning wasn't going to keep it cool.

"It's supposed to be fall, but I'll be glad when the temperature starts to drop."

"Still got a ways to go before then."

They worked in silence for a few minutes. "When do you think Charley is going to show up?" Vic asked.

## APPLE-ACHIAN TREASURE

Erin straightened and looked at her. "Are you trying to get me to badmouth my new boss?"

"She isn't your boss, she's your partner."

"I'd like to think so," Erin said slowly, "but I don't think that's the way she sees it. If we can't agree on things, who do you think is going to get the final say?"

"You're partners. You'll work it out together."

Erin shrugged. That remained to be seen.

"So…?" Vic pressed.

"I think we'll be lucky to see her before noon."

Vic giggled. "How about a bet? If she gets in before noon, you win. After noon, I win."

"And what do we win?"

"How about… a foot massage."

Erin shook her head. "Okay. You're on."

Charley didn't make it in before noon. Vic was chuckling to herself.

"I'm looking forward to that foot rub," she commented.

"I did say we'd be lucky to see her before noon. I hope nothing happened to her…"

"Nothing happened to her. She's just sleeping, like every day."

"I know… I just worry."

"She's fine. She said she was going to be here, but she hasn't got the sense of a cross-eyed goose. She's just like a kid. She's going to have to grow up if she's going to run a business."

Erin raised her eyebrows. Vic herself was barely an adult.

"I'm grown up," Vic shot at her. "It doesn't have anything to do with chronological age."

"No, you're right. She may be a few years older; she may even have been on her own for longer than you have, but she doesn't have the same sense of responsibility."

Vic nodded. There were parallels between Vic and Charley. Both had left home at an early age, rebelling against the way that they had been raised. But Charley had left, apparently, because she wanted a more exciting life on the opposite side of the law, and Vic had come out about her gender identity, transitioning to female. Despite her not aligning herself with the gender she'd been raised as, Vic still had strong moral standards and an attachment to her family. They were the ones who had forced her to leave. Erin was glad that Jeremy, one of Vic's older brothers, had recently moved into town. It was good for Vic to have contact with someone in her family. Jeremy accepted her for who she was and did his best to respect her identity.

"Think she'll show up after lunch?" Erin asked.

"Do you want to go double or nothing?"

"No. Just wondering. It's opening day, you'd think she'd at least make an appearance."

"You would think," Vic agreed.

Mary Lou and Melissa arrived together. Erin was glad to see them together more often again lately. Mary Lou needed the support of her friends more than ever, and Erin suspected that Melissa wasn't having the easiest time since she had started visiting Davis in prison. The ladies of Bald Eagle Falls were not very tolerant of what they perceived as wrong choices.

Mary Lou looked around the bakery and raised her brows. "I was expecting a better turnout for your opening day. Isn't this a little… quiet…?"

Erin shrugged, her face getting warm. "We actually didn't want to do a great big grand reopening. We didn't think it was a good idea, after…"

Mary Lou gazed at her blankly.

"Because of the deaths," Melissa piped up eagerly. "Angela was killed on opening day of Auntie Clem's Bakery and Mr. Inglethorpe was killed the night before the grand reopening for The Bake Shoppe. Were you afraid of jinxing it?"

"No," Erin insisted, though she had to admit to a little superstitious twinge over the thought of another murder around the bakery opening. So far everything had been quiet, and she hoped that it would stay that way. They didn't need any bodies to spice things up. "I just didn't want people to make that association." She looked significantly at the other patrons of the bakery, hoping that Melissa would get the hint and keep her voice down. "Even if it's unconscious… I didn't want them to think… bakery opening… someone might die…"

"That makes perfect sense," Mary Lou acknowledged.

"It's really too bad, though," Melissa said. "I wouldn't mind a free muffin…"

Erin smiled. "You buy a dozen for the Police Department, and I'll throw in a free one for you."

"You'd do that anyway."

Mary Lou and Melissa looked through the case at the baked goods on offer.

"I think… a loaf of the rustic bread," Mary Lou pointed to a hand-shaped loaf. "That would go nicely with supper. And maybe some cookies that I can throw in the freezer. We don't go through them very fast, with it just being Josh and I now, but we are starting to get a little low."

"Anything in particular, or just an assortment?" Erin asked.

"Surprise me."

Erin suspected that Mary Lou wasn't going to be eating any of them anyway. She was very careful to maintain her slim figure. Josh, on the other hand, was a teenager and could probably put away the whole dozen in a sitting without consequences.

"How are the boys?" she asked politely.

"As well as can be expected. Josh is finding high school very challenging. And Campbell… well, I don't know what to think of Campbell. He at least calls me once every week or so, which is more than one can expect from a boy his age. He says he's well, that things are going fine… but he's not going anywhere. I don't even know how he's supporting himself without any marketable skills."

"You don't know what he's doing?"

Mary Lou shook her head. "He's *finding himself.* Whatever that means."

Erin wasn't sure how to respond to that. She finished assembling the cookies for Mary Lou and handed them over to Vic to ring up at the till. She looked at Melissa. "So, a dozen muffins?"

"No, not today. Maybe on Friday. How about…" Melissa studied the display case seriously. "How about a brownie?" She motioned to the chocolate-dipped brownies that Erin had recently added to the product lineup. "Those are addictive. They should be a controlled substance."

Erin nodded. "You'd better not tell Officer Piper that. I don't want him slapping me with any fines. Or jail time."

Melissa gave one of her wide smiles, her eyes dancing. "What you and Officer Piper do behind closed doors really isn't any of my business…"

For the second time, Erin felt a wave of heat go over her face, and was sure that this time she was turning a brilliant red. She shouldn't let Melissa get to her like that. Blushing would only encourage her in the future. But she couldn't keep a dispassionate mask when she thought about Terry Piper and their relationship. They had only recently taken things to the next level with the good-looking officer, and Erin wasn't to the point where she could be casual about it.

"You mind your manners," Vic drawled, her southern accent more pronounced than usual. "Don't be teasing Miss Erin or she'll be adding something to your tea this Sunday."

## APPLE-ACHIAN TREASURE

Melissa responded with a blush of her own. She tittered and gave Vic the money to cover her bill. "I don't know what you're talking about, I'm sure."

It wouldn't have been so bad if Officer Handsome himself hadn't happened to enter the bakery at that very moment.

The bells jingled as Terry walked in the front door, K9 poised at his side in perfect form, as usual. Erin's heart skipped a beat at the sight of her sweetheart in uniform, but she was already embarrassed by Melissa's comments and couldn't help but feel even more awkward at his appearance on the scene. She glanced over at Vic.

"I uh, just have to go check on those cookies. Can you get K9 a biscuit and see what Terry wants? I'll be right back!"

Vic looked surprised. Erin turned tail and dashed into the kitchen, needing to get out of sight to compose herself. She ran cold water into a clean cloth and pressed it to her cheeks, trying to cool them off and remove the color. Terry would be wondering what she was so flushed about.

Not like he wouldn't wonder why she had suddenly fled at his appearance. That wasn't something she normally did.

Erin took an extra few seconds to gulp down a glass of water, then returned to the front before everyone could start to wonder what had happened to her. But that last swallow water went down wrong and she inhaled half of it into her windpipe, resulting in a fit of coughing just as she walked through the door. If she'd been trying for an unobtrusive re-entrance, she had not succeeded.

Erin turned away, coughing into her elbow, and then turned back, her face just as hot as it had been when she'd left.

"Sorry. I'm not contagious. Just some water that went down the wrong way."

"Are you okay?" Terry asked, looking concerned.

"I'm fine, really. Just some water." Erin cleared her throat the best she could, trying to suppress any further coughs. "How are you today?"

"It's a beautiful day out. Things have been pretty quiet. I'm hoping that the crime level in Bald Eagle Falls has gone back to normal."

"You think that the trouble with the clans is done?"

"Considering the fact that we managed to confiscate several millions of dollars' worth of drugs, hopefully they've decided that Bald Eagle Falls isn't the best place for a storage and shipping depot, and we won't be seeing any more of them."

"I sure hope so," Erin said fervently.

Terry nodded. "How has the first day back been?"

Erin breathed out. She blinked to clear her teary eyes and studied the officer. Taller than she was, dark haired, perfect build, and that cute little dimple in his cheek when he smiled at her. "Actually, it's been pretty nice. It felt good to get back into the routine again. When I wasn't working, it just felt… disorderly. I didn't feel like my life was going the way I wanted it to. Like things might just fall apart at any minute."

"But coming back, everything has fallen back into the old patterns?"

Erin nodded. "It feels good."

"It actually does," Vic agreed. "Unlike Erin, I actually enjoyed my time off, but I was ready to come back. The structure and the routine are good, but even more than that… the paycheck… visiting with customers… eating at regular intervals instead of grazing all day." Vic patted her flat belly. "I was starting to put on weight…"

"You were not," Erin disagreed. "You haven't put on an ounce since you moved here."

"Well, that's not exactly true. But considering I wasn't getting enough to eat before I started working for you, those

## APPLE-ACHIAN TREASURE

first few ounces were okay. It's the ones since then that are the problem."

Erin just shook her head.

"See you later, Officer Piper," Melissa gave Terry a little wave before leaving. She did some office administration for the Police Department on a part-time basis, and quite enjoyed the prestige of her role, even if she wasn't an officer herself.

Terry nodded to her and Mary Lou as they headed out the door. "Ladies."

They were just coming up on the after-school rush when Charley finally showed her face. She rushed into the bakery through the front door, red-faced and flustered.

"I can't believe how the day has gotten away from me!" she exclaimed. "I was just doing some administrative work from home, you know, making sure that all of the advertising is lined up and that the bank has made all of the appropriate arrangements and all that…" All work that Erin had already attended to herself. "And before I knew it, it's afternoon and I still haven't made it over to the bakery! How did it go? Do you need anything?"

They were, of course, long past the point that Charley could have helped with anything, unless she wanted to take over the register during the rush or help with the cleanup after closing. Erin just looked at her.

"I was working," Charley insisted. "I was just doing it from home instead of here. It's so hot in the kitchen and that little office…"

The office was bigger than the one Erin had used in the original Auntie Clem's Bakery, which had been hardly more than a closet. With a desk fan on the heat was nearly tolerable.

"I didn't say anything," she asserted. "Things went pretty well. We had a good amount of business."

"Good. I was a little worried after we decided not to do a big grand reopening. I mean, I didn't *want* to do a big reopening, I just had some… last minute qualms. What if nobody came? What if not enough people knew that we were open for business again today…?"

"There's nothing that says you have to make all of your money the first day," Erin reassured her. "Even if opening day didn't go well, there's lots of time for word to get around that we're open and to get people in. But, nothing to worry about, it went just fine."

"Good." Charley put a stuffed shoulder bag that doubled as her briefcase down on one of the little wrought iron tables at the front of the bakery. "I'm new to this whole 'business owner' thing. I don't want to screw it up."

"That's why you've got us," Vic offered, putting her arm around Erin's shoulder to remind Charley that she was there too, part of a package deal. "We know how to run a bakery."

Charley didn't quite make a face, but her look at Vic didn't convey that she was thankful to have Vic there helping to look after things. She and Vic had never quite clicked. Erin wasn't sure whether it was a personality thing, or whether there was a certain amount of jealousy between her sister and her best friend, each of them wary of the other intruding on their relationship with Erin.

"I'm glad I've got you," Charley agreed, but her words were aimed at Erin rather than at Vic. "Whenever I start to panic about not knowing everything there is to know about the business, I just remind myself that you've done all of this before. I can't imagine how difficult it must have been for you to start up Auntie Clem's Bakery with no one to tell you how to do everything. How did you manage?"

Erin motioned Charley to move to the side so that she wasn't blocking paying customers.

"I read lots. Talked to my lawyer and accountant. Wrote out my business plan and goals and milestones…"

## APPLE-ACHIAN TREASURE

"You're so organized. You always know exactly what's coming next, don't you?"

Erin only wished that were true.

# Chapter Two

WHEN THEY ARRIVED HOME after closing the bakery, Erin saw that Rohilda Beaven's big white truck was parked in front of the house.

"Looks like Jeremy has company," she observed, and pulled around to the back to park in the garage.

"It's amazing how well they get on together," Vic said, shaking her head. "You'd think that with Beaver being older than him and a federal agent, they wouldn't have anything in common. But they get along like a house on fire!"

Erin winced at the expression. They had almost lost the house to fire once, and the original Auntie Clem's Bakery burning down was still too recent and a sore spot.

"Or like something on fire," Vic amended quickly, then tried again. "Or... like a pig and mud. They belong together!"

"They really have seemed to hit it off," Erin agreed. She unlocked the back door, pausing and calling out to warn Jeremy and Beaver that they were no longer alone. "We're home, Jeremy!"

They could hear the murmur of voices for a moment, then Jeremy's door opened, and he entered the kitchen.

"Hey Erin, hey Vic. How was the first day back?"

"It was good," Vic offered, giving him a quick hug. "Beaver's here?"

"She'll be out in a minute. We're just getting things packed up and ready to go."

## APPLE-ACHIAN TREASURE

Erin felt a little pang at the thought of Jeremy moving out. It had sometimes been awkward with him there, especially when he had been trying to hide out from the clans and the police. She had told him that he needed to find his own place, but she still felt responsible for him and like she might be turning him out of the nest too quickly.

"Everything is arranged at the new place?" she asked.

"Deposit and first month have been paid," Jeremy agreed. "So, it looks like I'm all grown up after all. My first place all my own."

Erin suspected that most of the money for the basement suite had been put up by Beaver, since Jeremy had just recently landed a job and hadn't likely received an advance on his paycheck. But he hadn't told her what arrangements were being made and it wasn't any of her business how he had managed to rent a place so quickly.

"It will be nice for you," Erin said. "You won't have me and all of the critters underfoot."

Orange Blossom, Erin's cat, was rubbing up against her legs meowing noisily over their conversation. Marshmallow was closer to Jeremy, and he bent down and picked up the brown and white rabbit. Marshmallow kicked his back legs, not liking to be lifted into the air, but Jeremy held the rabbit snug against his body and settled him down.

"Actually, I'm going to miss these guys. The house never seemed lonely with them around. My apartment is going to seem awfully quiet after being used to them running around here."

Erin wasn't about to offer that he could take one of them with him. She wouldn't be able to bear to part with either of them and would never separate the two. The cat and rabbit had grown remarkably close to each other.

Jeremy's bedroom door opened again, and Rohilda joined them in the kitchen. Her tall, lanky body, which always gave the impression of being slow and lazy, was anything but. She was strong quick, and graceful. She just conserved her energy until she had a need for it. She gave them a smile, chewing on a wad of gum. Her nose and lips were too big for her face and her blond hair was more like Jeremy's unruly mane than Vic's sleek, smooth hair. All together, she was not unattractive, but didn't have the type of beauty that society typically worshiped.

Erin had learned to appreciate her open, honest manner. Unlike the women of Bald Eagle Falls, whom Erin found difficult to read, with Beaver what you saw was what you got. She never put on a false front.

"Good evening," she greeted Erin and Vic. "Uneventful day at the bakery?"

Erin nodded vigorously. "Luckily, yes! I don't know what I would have done if… something… had happened. I might have a breakdown and never recover."

"Good thing we didn't have to find out."

"So…" Vic looked at Jeremy and back at Beaver. "I guess you're leaving tonight…?"

"Everything is packed up and ready to go," Beaver agreed. "Jer can sleep in his own bed tonight. I need to go back to the city for a few days, so he'll have some time to settle into his new digs. I'll be back for a day or two on the weekend." She looked at Jeremy with affection.

He grinned back at her. "I told her she could stay, but she doesn't want the commute. So, I guess I just get a few days here and there whenever she can fit me in. I feel used."

"You'd better not complain," Vic warned. "The lady is good with a gun."

Beaver grinned and nodded, chewing on her gum.

"I'm not complaining," Jeremy assured her, and put his arm around Beaver to pull her close for a moment. "I'm perfectly happy with being used."

Beaver laughed and gave him an embarrassingly passionate kiss. Erin looked at Vic and rolled her eyes.

"Did you work today?" Vic asked without waiting for Jeremy and Beaver to finish.

# APPLE-ACHIAN TREASURE

Jeremy pulled back from Beaver. "Yep. I don't work the long hours you two do, but I put in my time."

"What exactly is it that you're doing?" Erin asked. While he'd told her before, she never felt like she'd gotten a full explanation.

"Just keeping an eye on things," Jeremy said. "Making sure that no one bothers the crops."

Erin studied him, trying to make sense of the explanation. She knew that he was working on Crosswood Farm, but he had refused to tell what kind of crop he was guarding. It didn't seem likely that it was any of the crops that were widely farmed in the area. After all, why would fields need to be guarded against intruders? There was no reason for people to come in and steal corn or apples. What was the benefit, unless they were starving? It was harvest time, so the plants would be mature, but she couldn't see why anyone would be interested. Was there a black market for cider?

She was afraid that what he was doing wasn't quite as innocent as he made it sound.

Terry had said that they had eradicated the drug trade in Bald Eagle Falls, so Erin told herself it couldn't be anything to do with the clans. Jeremy had done his best to get away from the Jackson clan that he'd been born into. She couldn't see him giving in and just going right back to a life of crime. And she couldn't see Beaver letting him. Beaver didn't contradict anything Jeremy had said about his job, so either she knew the details, or she was satisfied that as much as he had said was the truth.

It just didn't make any sense to Erin.

"You've got to be on the lookout for poachers," Jeremy told Erin, watching her face carefully. "You'd be surprised at how much illegal trade there is around here."

"Poachers… so does that mean you are guarding animals? Not plants?"

He kept his face carefully blank. "I'm not allowed to talk about it."

"Not allowed to?"

"It's in my employment contract."

"So, your job is watching to make sure nobody steals a bunch of plants?"

He shrugged.

Erin looked at Beaver again, trying to read her expression, but she was even more closeted than Jeremy, giving Erin a cheeky smile that betrayed nothing of what she knew or didn't know about Jeremy's new job.

# Chapter Three

IN THE AFTERMATH OF the fire at old Auntie Clem's and the opening of the new bakery, Erin hadn't had time for much other than business arrangements. Even when she took some downtime to relax, it was usually to bake and experiment with new recipe possibilities.

Now that the bakery was open once more, she couldn't bring her brain to focus on anything else business-related, so Erin instead pulled out one of Clementine's fat genealogy files and started to leaf through it for old stories about Bald Eagle Falls and its residents. She'd never been much of a fiction reader, but she found history fascinating, and the stories of the old Bald Eagles Falls residents, progenitors of Erin and her friends, were particularly enthralling. They were people who had lived right there, had established the traditions that became ingrained in Bald Eagle Falls life, and had passed on names and physical and personality traits to the people Erin knew.

She carefully unfolded yellowing old newspaper articles, the dust tickling her nose, and dug up the past lives of Bald Eagle Falls. It was almost voyeuristic. She read in fascination about the ways they had lived and died. Where there were pictures, she studied them closely, sometimes with a magnifying glass, searching for familiar features and taking in the old-fashioned clothing and equipment. It must have been an interesting—and difficult—time to live.

She opened up a letter written on thick paper that had been folded twice, the paper almost brown with age. The old-fashioned cursive writing was difficult to read, but she was getting better at it after puzzling through dozens of letters. This one appeared not to be a letter, but a poem.

> The treasure it enfolds
> Where lies there forest gold
> A king's ransom hid amidst
> The warrens of the moles
> The gift of life to those who toil
> Each day to reap the sterile soil
> Be wise if thou would life preserve
> And no lord be forced to serve

Erin read over it a few times. She felt a thrill of excitement.

She tapped out a quick text to Vic.

*Do you want to find a treasure?*

It was a few minutes before Vic messaged her back a questioning smiley face. Erin grinned.

*Come and see!*

She looked out the attic window toward the apartment loft over the garage, where Vic's light was still turned on. In a few moments, she saw Vic's door open and saw the girl silhouetted against the light from inside for a moment before she hurried down the stairs and headed toward the house. Erin picked up the poem and went down the attic stairs to meet Vic in the kitchen. Vic stopped for a moment to make sure the burglar alarm hadn't been armed yet, then turned to look at Erin.

"A treasure? What's all this?"

Erin held the paper out to her, and Vic took it carefully by the edges. She didn't have as much practice as Erin did in reading the old-style script, so it took her a few minutes to

# APPLE-ACHIAN TREASURE

puzzle through the short poem, then she looked at Erin, eyes sparkling.

"Gold? Where did you find this? And how do you know it wasn't already found a hundred years ago?"

"We'd have to do some more research before we'd know one way or the other. Go through the rest of the file, the newspaper archives, see if there's anyone around who can remember what it's all about. I just thought..." Erin shrugged. "It sounded like fun. I've never had a real-life treasure to find before."

"And we needed another mystery to solve since no one was killed at the opening," Vic teased. "You might get bored without something to challenge that noggin of yours."

Erin rolled her eyes. "Honestly, what I need is something to take my mind off of Charley and whatever her next idea is going to be. This looked... promising."

"Forest gold," Vic said slowly, meditating on it. "A king's ransom. That's got to be pretty big. I mean, we're not just talking a few coins, here."

"Yeah. It has to be something good. Everyone says there is treasure hidden around here, right? Well... maybe there is. What if we could find it?"

"That would solve a lot of problems. Nothing like a little gold to smooth your way."

"So, you want to find out more?"

"Why don't we look through the file? We can do that tonight without having to go to anyone else or go to the library."

"It's upstairs. I'll go get it."

Vic was waiting on the couch when Erin brought the bulging file down the stairs. She laid it on the coffee table, being careful to keep everything in order and not let the papers spill out in an avalanche.

"It's like an archeological dig," she said. "Everything related to the poem should be in the layers around it, so we don't want to get them out of order."

"Right here in the middle?" Vic indicated the two stacks of paper. "I guess I'll take the top, and you can go through the bottom. You've already looked through the top anyway, haven't you?"

"Yes. You're sure you don't want to go through the bottom together? I don't think there was anything about treasure in that half."

"No, you go ahead and take the bottom. If there's anything about a hidden fortune or a treasure map in the top, I'll find it."

Erin shrugged. "Okay."

She took her half, and they started to go through the piles a page at a time. Orange Blossom had been sleeping on the arm of the easy chair but, hearing the rustling of paper, he woke up, stretched his body out slowly, and wandered over to see what they were looking at, making inquiring noises.

"Nothing interesting to kitties," Erin said, pushing him away with her toe. "Just boring old papers."

He went around her foot and approached Vic's pile. Vic pulled them away. "Nope. Not today, Mr. Blossom. I need to look at these."

Orange Blossom jumped up on the coffee table, sniffing all around the empty file folder. He sneezed three times, shaking his head briskly between each sneeze.

"Oh, gross!" Vic protested. "He sprayed cat snot on my papers!"

"Oops," Erin laughed. "I don't imagine that's good for them."

"If the oils from our skin and the acid in the paper can make it degrade, I hate to think of what cat snot could do."

Vic did the best to dab at the wet spots with a tissue and waved the papers in the air to dry them out.

"Have you found anything about the treasure?" Erin asked.

## APPLE-ACHIAN TREASURE

"No, not yet. Just lots of marriage and death records and what dresses everyone is wearing to what parties." She sighed. "Were people really so shallow? That's all they had to put in the newspaper?"

"Well, it isn't like today when we can gather news from all over the world. They probably didn't even hear much from outside the county. It was all local news. So, the social stuff became really important."

Vic shook her head. "I love a nice party dress as much as the next girl, but this is going a bit too far, if you ask me."

Erin looked at the additional articles she had read through. "There's a bunch of war stuff too. You don't really think about how it affected people out here in the hills. You think they were far away from the fighting, and their lives would just go on as normal. But people from all over sent their sons to fight, and the war disrupted all kinds of infrastructure and people's ability to earn money. It's no wonder someone would write about finding treasure to save your life and not have to serve anyone else. It sounds like things were pretty grim."

"I guess it must have been important to keep up appearances," Vic said, fingering through her social notices, "even if they were dirt-poor and having trouble making ends meet."

"I guess."

"Did you find anything else about the treasure?"

"I don't know." Erin had her fingers marking a couple of places in the file. "This one talks about people trying to solve a riddle. And this one talks about them waiting for gold to come in to pay for shipments of corn that had been sent to the front."

"Maybe related and maybe not," Vic agreed.

She pushed Orange Blossom off the coffee table in order to put her pile of papers back into the file folder. He landed awkwardly on his back, flipped over, and jumped to his feet. He licked down the fur on his back and glared at Vic.

Erin laughed. "Stay out of the way and you won't get pushed off."

Vic looked toward the back of the house and Erin heard the growl of a truck engine a moment later.

"That will be Willie," Vic said. "We'd better head to bed if we're going to be up in time in the morning."

"Okay. Say 'hi' to Willie for me."

"He says 'hi' back," Vic said. She gave Erin a quick hug around the shoulders and headed out. "I'll arm the alarm," she called back to Erin.

"Okay. Thanks."

Erin put her papers back into the folder. "And off to bed for us too," she told Orange Blossom. He immediately took a few steps toward the kitchen doorway and looked back at her expectantly. Erin followed him and, as soon as she was in the kitchen, she heard the patter of Marshmallow's paws behind her. She gave them each their treats and shut off the lights.

"We should ask Beaver for her thoughts on the hidden treasure," Vic suggested to Erin while they prepared the baking the next morning. "She's the one experienced at this kind of thing."

Erin thought about it. "I guess that would be okay," she agreed. "I don't think she's the kind of person who would take off on her own to claim it for herself, do you?"

"No." Vic considered the matter herself. "I know treasure hunters are known for having no honor… but I think Beaver does. It isn't like she took all the credit for the drug bust, did she? She could have. She could have said it was all her doing."

Erin had been thinking the same thing. "We could ask Terry what he thinks."

"You're going to tell Terry?"

## APPLE-ACHIAN TREASURE

"Of course!" Erin was surprised Vic would even ask. "Why wouldn't I?"

"I just wondered… he might not like you… you know… detecting."

"It's not detecting. Not like asking about a murder. I'm just… looking into something from the past. Genealogy. He won't care. There's nothing dangerous about it."

Terry didn't welcome the idea quite as much as Erin had hoped he would. His mouth formed a straight line and his forehead creased as he thought about it.

"It's just an old poem," Erin said. "I'm sure it probably won't even lead to anything; it's just something sort of fun to look into. It's not like it's a crime. It's not something dangerous."

"I'd agree, except that I know the way you seem to stir things up… just because you don't think there's anything to it or anything to worry about, that doesn't mean it's true. You seem to have a knack for finding dangerous things, even if it doesn't seem like there would be anything to it. Treasure maps and hidden tunnels… they shouldn't be real… but they are."

Erin tried to shrug it off.

"I really don't think this is anything that's going to attract any attention. We'll keep it quiet. Just me and Vic."

"And Jeremy and Beaver. And whoever else you happen to ask for background information from. Maybe the librarian."

"And you, but you're not going to suddenly turn into a homicidal maniac, are you?"

He didn't crack a smile at her teasing, which told Erin that he really was worried.

"Really, it's just a poem," she said. "It will probably turn out to be something some high school student wrote for an English assignment. You really think there is a chest of gold buried out there in the forest somewhere?"

"No… but people can act strangely when they think there is. You don't know how people might react to the suggestion that there's a treasure to be found. What happened when you told people that there was a locked cabinet in your basement that might hold some kind of key to finding an ancient pirate treasure?"

"Well… someone broke in." Erin hadn't even thought about that. They would have to be careful of security and make sure they didn't tell the wrong person what they were looking for. "I'll be careful, Terry, but I really don't think you have anything to worry about."

Terry sighed and shook his head. "Famous last words."

# Chapter Four

In spite of Terry's concerns, Erin forged on ahead. She agreed that they would need to make sure that the wrong people didn't find out about the poem and what they were looking for, but she still wanted to find out more about the poem, who wrote it, and what the treasure was that was possibly hidden somewhere in the forest. What were the chances that it was still there after so many years? If it had even existed, the chances that it would still be there were, Erin thought, pretty slim. But it would be fun to try to find out anyway. Like geocaching, it would be fun just to see where the clues led them, even if they didn't find anything that had intrinsic value.

They decided to have supper with Beaver and Jeremy at the Chinese restaurant and, after eating, Erin pulled out the poem, which she had carefully protected in a plastic sleeve and transported in a clipboard to make sure it didn't get folded, crushed, or torn. Erin gave a little preamble about looking through Clementine's genealogy, then handed the poem across the table to Beaver and Jeremy to have a look at.

Beaver's eyes gleamed as she read through the poem. Her smile was wider than ever. She passed it over to Jeremy for him to read. "Got the treasure-hunting bug?" she asked Erin. "This looks like a lot of fun."

"Do you think it's real?"

"If you didn't make it up, it's real. But a real what, we don't know. Is it actually a clue to a treasure? A real treasure? Something that is still valuable today? And if it is, has that treasure been found, or is it still out there? How many people know about it? How many people have looked for it? What are the chances it has been found?"

"Well, I guess the chances are pretty good that it might have been," Erin said, shifting uncomfortably. "I mean, it's been a long time, so someone might have found it just by accident, not even looking for it. And if a lot of people know that it exists or have looked for it…"

"Right," Beaver nodded. "Don't get your hopes up too much. There is no guarantee that this treasure is even around anymore. If there is a treasure. It could just be a poem."

Erin nodded.

"Was there anything else with it? Something that might indicate that it is legitimate?"

"It was in a folder with a lot of other stuff, but none of the other papers I went through mention it at all. So, I don't know… I found some other newspaper clippings that might be related."

Erin withdrew the other clippings from her clipboard, likewise preserved in plastic sleeves to keep them from tearing or being damaged.

Beaver took the other two articles and read them through slowly. She pursed her generous lips, thinking it through.

"You're right," she agreed. "They could be related or could be nothing to do with the poem. You could just be making connections between things that are completely unrelated to each other. It's pretty tenuous." She looked at them again. "Solving a riddle… it could just be some kind of crossword or brain teaser that the paper had published the previous week. There might have been a prize for being able to crack the code. If it was related to your poem, then

## APPLE-ACHIAN TREASURE

they might have figured out what it meant a hundred and fifty years ago. Do your newspaper archives go back that far?"

Erin shook her head. "I haven't looked yet, but I doubt it. Though Aunt Clementine got this from somewhere. Someone still had old newspapers around twenty years ago when she was on a genealogy kick."

"This wasn't clipped from any official archives. It's original. If it was in archives, she would have done a microfiche print or photocopy. No archivist is going to let you clip out of the original paper."

"No," Erin agreed. "But Clementine had a lot of stuff that was original papers."

"She must have known someone who hoarded them. Or she had them herself from an ancestor's collection. Sometimes old papers were used as insulation in walls or attics. She might have come across it during some renovations."

"I don't know when it was she built the reading room in the attic. She could have found it then."

Beaver nodded. "You never know what you're going to find in old attics and crawlspaces."

"What's the other one?" Jeremy asked.

Beaver slid them over to him so that he could read them as well. Jeremy read over the description of the payment the town was awaiting for the crops that had been shipped out.

"How much would they have been expecting to get for one shipment of crops? It wouldn't have been a king's ransom. Just part of one year's earnings."

Fresh off the farm himself, Jeremy would have a pretty good idea of how that worked. "One portion of one year's crops wouldn't even be enough for the farmers to get through one year. It certainly wouldn't set anyone up for life."

"No, I guess not," Erin admitted, with a twinge of disappointment.

"A king's ransom might well be an exaggeration," Beaver said. "If it *was* the payment for the crops that was lost or hidden, it might still be worth quite a lot… just not as much as you would hope."

"Or it might be practically worthless," Vic put in. "We don't know how big this crop was that they sent to the troops, how many farms it was from. If it was just one or two farms, then we could be talking about ten bucks each for the laborers."

"Gold is still worth something, though," Erin argued. "Ten dollars of gold a hundred and fifty years ago would be what now?"

Beaver gave a grin. "It would still have some value. Especially since we don't have to pay anybody's wages with it this many years later." She took a sip of her green tea. "I just don't want you getting your hopes up. You might think that because you found a tunnel full of illegal drugs on your first try that treasure hunting is easy, and it's not. I've looked for a lot of treasures over the years, and I've only been successful in a handful of cases. Enough to keep me looking for more, but the actual value of what I have found so far doesn't amount to even a fraction of a king's ransom. If you're looking for this, it should be because of the challenge, not because you think you're actually going to make a fortune."

Erin nodded. "To be honest, I just want something to do that isn't related to the bakery and Charley. I want a diversion. Reading through genealogy stories is fun, but this is even better… I kind of like solving puzzles."

"Kind of," Vic agreed with a wry grin. "What did Officer Piper have to say about it, by the way?"

"It's just a poem," Erin said, not answering the question. "There's no harm in seeing if we can figure it out."

"Well," Beaver positioned the poem in front of herself again, reading it through. "With the mention of moles, I'd say our first clue leads to an underground tunnel. Now you

## APPLE-ACHIAN TREASURE

wouldn't know anything about underground tunnels in these parts, would you?"

Erin laughed. "Well, it's not in the tunnel under the bakery, I can tell you that. I think the DEA would have mentioned if they'd found a stash of gold down there with the drugs."

"Or else the Jackson clan made off with it when they first discovered the tunnel," Beaver agreed, "and if they did, they're not very likely to share that news with us."

"But what are the chances that it would have been hidden in that tunnel? Or in any of the old tunnels that were right in town? If it was you, wouldn't you hide it somewhere more remote? I wouldn't want people stumbling over it here in town. If those tunnels were used regularly during the war, then they would have been too well-known to hide anything really valuable. You wouldn't want some other person in town just stumbling across the treasure."

Beaver nodded. "You're probably right. Though we don't know how many people knew about the tunnels, or if they knew about all of them, or if each family only knew about the ones that were connected to their homes or businesses. There were probably some tunnels that were only known to the owner."

"So, you think we should try to find as many of the old tunnels in town as we can?"

"No."

Everybody just looked at Beaver. She took a long sip of her tea and grinned at Jeremy.

"I think that after the big drug bust, everybody is looking for signs of tunnels under their houses and workplaces. It isn't exactly a secret anymore. One thing you need to know about treasure hunting is that if you look in the same places everybody else is looking, you're not going to find anything. It would be a waste of time for us to go around town trying to find all of the old tunnels. Everybody else is already doing that, and they've either found a tunnel and aren't going to tell you about it, or they don't want anyone looking for tunnels on their property. They're not just going to invite you in to look at their basements while you try to catalog all of the old tunnels in Bald Eagle Falls."

"We could make it into a contest," Vic suggested. "We could have everybody who has found a tunnel make a submission to a contest, and then the person we draw or the person who knows the most about the old tunnel system wins a prize…"

"Of what? A gluten-free muffin? Nobody is going to tell you about their secret tunnels for even a full box of muffins."

"The town could enact some kind of law that all of the tunnels have to be registered," Jeremy suggested. "For safety reasons. An inspector has to go check out each one to make sure that it is safe and isn't going to collapse. Then there would be a record of where they all were, and we'd probably be able to find a few new ones that hadn't been discovered yet between dead-end tunnels…"

Beaver was shaking her head. "None of that would be of any help to us. Like I said, you're just looking where other people have already been. There's no point. And even if you did get the town to enact a law like that, most people would decide that their secret tunnels were their own business and they'd refuse to register them. You wouldn't even get enough votes on the town council to pass a law like that."

"Let's assume it's not in the townsite," Vic said. "Like Beaver says, everybody is already looking for those tunnels. There are plenty of places outside the townsite a treasure could have been hidden. It's not necessarily a man-made tunnel. It could be a natural cave or a mine."

Erin gave a shudder.

"You wouldn't happen to know anyone who is an expert on caves around here, would you?" Beaver asked with a grin.

Willie had been invited to dinner, but he'd had other things to do and hadn't been able to join them. Erin hadn't

## APPLE-ACHIAN TREASURE

thought about him being a resource in their search for the treasure, or she would have tried to schedule a better time for their dinner so he would be able to join them. It made sense, when she thought about the "warrens of moles" in the poem that they should be looking for tunnels, caves, or mines. And that was Willie's purview.

"Do you think Willie would be able to help us?" Erin asked Vic.

"Sure. But you know... he's not the treasure hunting kind."

It seemed like a strange thing to say. Willie spent much of his time mining or exploring caves or old mine shafts, which sounded exactly like treasure hunting to Erin. Erin frowned at Vic.

"But... that's what he does."

"Mining isn't the same as treasure hunting," Vic disagreed. "It's science based. He knows which mines are more likely to produce because of the surrounding geology and what he's taken out of there before. Treasure hunting is... pretty much chance. If he agrees to help out, it will probably be for a fee. And not a portion of whatever you find, an up-front fee."

"Oh." Erin hadn't thought about that. Of course, she knew that Willie was involved in a wide variety of money-making ventures. He wasn't the kind of guy who was satisfied working one job and making a regular salary. He followed his interests and did a lot of smaller jobs on a short-term basis. If he were going to waste time looking for treasures in caves, then of course it would be for a fee. He wasn't going to take time out of paying jobs for something that was just for a favor. "Yeah, that makes sense. We'll have to talk to him about what his fee would be."

"If you're just doing it for fun, you don't want to be pouring money into the venture," Beaver warned. "If Willie doesn't want to help just for the challenge, you might not want to run up your costs. There are bound to be other people who have some knowledge of caves in the area, old survey maps, things like that."

"Yeah." The wind had been taken out of Erin's sails a little. She had hoped that she would be able to figure out the clues to where the treasure might be with a little ingenuity and the help of her friends. She hadn't considered having to pay for professional advice. She looked down at the poem in front of Beaver. "So, what else? Do you think there are any other clues as to where it is in the poem? If it's supposed to direct us to the treasure, it doesn't seem like there are many things to point to a particular location."

"No, you're right. Talking about those who toil... that lends some credence to it being the lost payment for the corn crop... sterile soil, though... that could be something else. Some of the other words in the poem might be locator clues, too. King and lord are both named, so you might be looking for a location that is named after someone with high-ranking authority. Or for a castle-shaped landmark. Life preserve... I don't suppose they had any animal preserves back then... but I might look into whether there were any endangered species they were trying to protect."

Erin jotted words down on her napkin, listing the clues and then places or ideas that came to her mind. Her excitement started to rise again. "I'm going to need some maps. And to do some more research on the area around here. And there might be something in the clippings Clementine kept about royalty; I wasn't looking for that..."

# Chapter Five

RELAXING AFTER A LONG day of work at the bakery and butting heads with Charley, Erin decided to let the animals out for a frolic in the back yard. They were pretty good about staying in the yard. Marshmallow sometimes attempted to burrow out under the fence and Orange Blossom sometimes jumped up on top of it, but when Erin told him to cut it out or she wouldn't let him out in the yard again, he would jump down, glaring at her, and go eat the longer grass at the back fence, which he would then throw up in the house. Marshmallow didn't pay any attention to her one way or the other, and it was just a matter of making sure any previous attempts to burrow were filled in and shooing him out whenever he tried to dig his way out again.

They were both happy exploring the smells of the large back yard and pretending they were out in the wild. Erin watched Orange Blossom stalking butterflies and grasshoppers, pretending he was a mighty hunter like his progenitors.

"Just don't bring me anything dead," she warned him, not wanting to be faced with any surprises if he happened to catch a mouse or vole.

His ear twitched at her words but, other than that, he ignored her and continued his hunt. Marshmallow had disappeared around the corner of the garage, so Erin got up to find him and shoo him back into the main part of the back yard where she could watch him.

As she approached the rabbit, she saw Adele coming down the worn path from the woods. Adele waited to make sure that Marshmallow wasn't going to make a break for it before she opened the gate to let herself in. But the rabbit seemed to be enthralled with whatever it was he had found growing beside the garage. Erin remembered that was just about where she had found him the first time, a young rabbit, injured by one of the pieces of equipment that had been clearing away the rubble of the old garage.

Erin waited until Adele was through the gate and had closed it again before giving Marshmallow another nudge.

"Come on, you. Come back to the yard where I can see you."

Marshmallow chewed on a plant, resisting her foot.

"Marshmallow. Come on, bunny. I don't know what you're eating, but it's probably not good for you. Come to the house and I'll give you a nice piece of apple."

He didn't move. Erin bent down and picked him up, wrapping her hands around his soft belly and picking him up to move him a few feet away. Marshmallow hopped back toward the house, acting as if he didn't care. Erin looked down at the plant he'd been grazing on. Yellow leaves and bright red berries.

"Do you know what this is?" she asked Adele. It wasn't one of the plants she recognized by sight. Granted, she only had a limited knowledge, but she knew most of the plants that grew around the house so that she could be sure the boys weren't poisoning themselves on whatever they were eating.

Adele took a few steps closer and crouched down. She didn't give any immediate sign of recognizing it.

"Maybe I should take a picture and look it up," Erin suggested.

## APPLE-ACHIAN TREASURE

Adele took another minute, then looked up. "You don't need to. It's wild ginseng."

"Ginseng?" Erin raised her brows and looked at it. She knew a little bit about ginseng from Clementine's stores of teas that Erin still served at the ladies' tea every Sunday. It was supposed to give energy and alertness, to help boost the immune system, and a whole host of other uses. Like some other herbs, the list of what ginseng might do was probably longer than the list of what it couldn't do.

Adele nodded. "You're very fortunate. Wild ginseng is a rare find these days. It used to be more plentiful, but it was over-harvested for the Asian market and just about disappeared from these mountains. The Chinese call it 'manroot' because of the shape of the roots. In these parts, they called it 'sang' and the people who made a living searching for it were called 'sangers.'"

"So, I shouldn't pull it," Erin suggested.

"Oh, no. I wouldn't do that. In fact, I'd suggest that you take these berries," Adele indicated the red, wrinkled berries, "and plant them in similar spots around the yard, then make sure the rabbit doesn't eat them when they come up."

"Can I use it? Like ginseng you would buy at the store? It's not toxic or anything?"

"No, it has many beneficial properties. If you're going to use it, may I make a suggestion…?"

"Sure, of course."

"A plant like this takes five to ten years to grow. It's just coming into maturity and the age that it can be legally harvested. Since it's in your own yard and you're using it for your own purposes, you don't need a license and you don't have to wait until it's ten years old, but if you were harvesting it for commercial purposes, there is a long list of regulations to adhere to. The part that you want to use is the root…" Adele pushed her finger down into the ground and followed the stem down underground and cleared soil away from the top part of the large, parsnip-like root. "This rhizome. If you were harvesting it commercially, you would dig up the whole thing, because the Asian market only wants intact roots, especially if it's the classic man shape. But if you're just using it for yourself, you don't need to sacrifice the whole plant. Just cut off an inch or two of the root, dry it, and use it as you wish. Leave the rest of it growing, plant all of the seeds it produces and, in a few years, you'll have a good crop of ginseng available."

Erin nodded. "Okay. I don't need to do anything special to treat the roots? Just dry them?"

"You can use fresh roots as well, especially for tea, but it is usually preserved by drying. Just wash and lay out in the sun, make sure it doesn't get moldy."

"And it's not going to hurt Marshmallow? Eating the leaves?"

"The leaves aren't normally used. Deer and rabbits eat them in the wild. It might make him a bit more frisky, but it won't hurt him."

## Chapter Six

WITH THE ANIMALS BACK where she could see both of them once more, Erin sat down in one of the outdoor chairs with Adele, and they watched the pets while relaxing in the fresh air.

"So… how is everything going?" Erin asked. "Is everything back to normal?"

Adele didn't answer for a while. She watched the animals, considering, and Erin wasn't sure whether she was going to attempt an answer. Adele looked up at the sky. Erin took a quick glance up to see if she could see Adele's pet crow, but she couldn't pick a black speck out in the blue sky and fluffy white clouds.

"I guess I'm waiting to see if everything goes back to normal," Adele said slowly. "In the past… things haven't turned out well when Rudolph has shown up. He has a way of attracting people's attention and making them uncomfortable."

He had done more than make people uncomfortable in the short time he had been in Bald Eagle Falls. But Erin kept that comment to herself. Adele knew as well as anyone what had happened. She didn't need to be reminded.

"He's a handsome guy," she commented. "I would imagine people notice him."

"If he was just handsome, that would be one thing," Adele said, nodding. "People might notice a good-looking guy, but then forget about him ten minutes later. But with his personality, his need to be the center of attention and to make sure everyone sees him and takes notice…"

Erin nodded. She had not been particularly comfortable around Rudolph. He had definitely come across as someone who was self-important, who expected people to do what he said because he was rich or had influence.

"Yeah. He does kind of come across that way."

"He has a lot of flaws. I never found much reason to stay with him… I was attracted to him, and things would go well for a while… but before long, he was looking at other women, hardly taking any notice of me at all, chasing these big deals or unsavory deals… and I would just get so fed up with him and cut him off."

"And then he'd come after you and you'd fall for him all over again?"

Adele made a face. "It makes me sound shallow. I knew we weren't good for each other, but when he would come after me…"

"I don't think it makes you shallow if you loved him. You can't just turn that off because you want to."

"There has to be more to a relationship than attraction. Falling in love is no excuse for staying with someone who is ultimately going to be bad for you. The whole idea of falling in love…"

Erin waited. Adele shook her head and puffed out her breath. "I don't know how to put it. Attraction isn't love, and the whole idea of falling in love just because you're physically attracted to someone… I guess I thought I was above that. I was better than that."

"We can't help how we feel."

"We can help how we act. It isn't enough to be physically attracted. There are people all over the world who don't act just because they are attracted to someone they see. If they're already married, or not social equals in their society, or there are other reasons that the relationship is a bad idea, people choose not to act on mere attraction. And it sounds simple. It sounds easy."

Erin watched Orange Blossom stalk a butterfly. "It sounds easy," she admitted. "It sounds like you should just be able to turn it off and make a better choice. But people all over the world make the wrong choice, too. It isn't that easy."

"No," Adele agreed with a sigh. "It isn't."

They were silent for a while. The breeze blew Clementine's wind chimes, and Erin listened to the soft musical background it produced.

"For what it's worth, I'm sorry," Erin told Adele. "I know this couldn't have been easy for you. You didn't ask him to show up and... do the stuff he did. And now people are acting like you were involved. When it didn't have anything to do with you."

"It doesn't matter where I went... sooner or later, he would get bored with his life or the affair or the sure thing that never panned out, and he would look for me again. I'd end up falling for him again, acting like a silly schoolgirl instead of like a grown woman with a mind of her own, letting him back into my life again, somehow thinking that things would be different this time. This time he would really mean it and he would stay, and things would work out between us. But that's not the way it worked. People don't change." She gave her head a bitter shake. "People never change."

Erin turned her head to look at Adele.

"Sometimes they do. If they really want to."

"The trouble with Rudolph is, whether that is true or not, is that he never wanted to. He never saw any reason to change."

Erin decided to give Charley a shot behind the counter for the ladies' tea on Sunday. Charley had made it to a few of the teas as a customer, so she knew what went on and was usually able to get herself out of bed and to get there in time. That would give both Vic and Bella the day off so they wouldn't have to pay for employee time. Charley wouldn't have to be there early for baking, as they generally prepared an assortment of cookies and treats ahead of time rather than baking on Sunday.

Charley arrived before church services let out to help Erin to arrange the trays and get everything prepared.

"Thanks for doing this today," Erin said, not sure how to say 'thanks for waking up on time' in a diplomatic way. "It's a nice break for Vic and Bella."

Charley nodded. "Sure, of course." She was a little flushed, and looked around as if she were sure she had forgotten something. Erin had been doing the ladies' teas enough times that they were now routine, but she recognized Charley's anxiety over getting everything set up right and presenting herself as a professional. "It's my place too, so I should be the public face at least part of the time."

"Don't worry, everything is fine," Erin assured her. "There isn't a lot to do for the tea. I do one big urn of black tea and make sure there's lots of hot water for anyone who wants a different blend or herbal tea. Everything else is prepared. The ladies just like to come and visit."

"It didn't seem like anything when you were doing it. But now that I'm partially responsible for seeing that everything runs smoothly…"

Erin nodded, chuckling. "Then it's a little bit different, isn't it? It will be just fine. If anybody needs anything, they'll ask."

Charley gulped. "Right. It will be just fine."

They worked on setting the treats out on trays. "I was wondering," Erin said, "what your family was like. Your adoptive family, I mean. You were with them right from the time you were a baby, right?"

It seemed strange to Erin that Charley had ended up being so rebellious when she'd been raised in a normal two-parent home her whole life. Erin understood kids like Reg ending up on the wrong side of the law. Multiple traumas, inconsistent parenting, no support system once they aged out of care; it was only natural for them to fall into street life, to be distrustful of anyone who tried to tell them what to do, and to scrape up what living they could by whatever means they could find. But Charley…

Charley looked at Erin for a moment, then went back to arranging sweets.

"Yeah, I've been with them for as long as I can remember," she agreed. "They picked me up at the hospital when I was just a few days old."

"And what are they like? What do your parents do?"

"They're good people… just your normal, everyday Joes. My dad does bodywork and my mom is a schoolteacher. Elementary school. Good, stable upbringing. Someone to help me if I ever ran into problems with my schoolwork. Good, loving influence." Charley flashed her a look. "So where did they go wrong, huh? Or is it just in the blood?"

"I didn't mean that. I just wondered… I don't know much about where you came from. I'd like to. You know about me."

Charley laughed and shook her head. "I know about you? Not much, Erin. Grew up in foster care. Inherited a bakery from your aunt. Started playing detective. It's not like you've divulged much to me about your life either."

Erin frowned. She checked on the tea, even though she knew it was just fine and didn't need any fiddling. "I've told you more than that."

"Really? Hmm… let's see. You have a foster sister named Reg. I know that because I met her. You had one named Caroline who died because she was celiac and wouldn't follow a gluten-free diet. And…? Have I missed something?"

"I was through a bunch of different homes," Erin said. "There isn't really one home that I consider my family or the one main influence on me. It was all pretty chaotic."

"How old were you when you went into care?"

"Eight." Erin was happy to have one question that was easy to answer. She hadn't expected the conversation to backfire on her. "Or, right before I turned eight. I was in foster care for my eighth birthday."

"So, you must remember something about your parents. About my birthmother."

"A little. It's not really clear. But some."

"So, what was she like? Did you bake with her? Is that where you got your love for cooking?"

"No... not that I remember. I don't think... I don't think baking was something she was ever interested in. I liked playing at the tea shop with Clementine. Maybe we baked cookies once or twice there. I don't remember much about my mother. Just... being around her. In the car. At home. Maybe... watching TV or cleaning..." Erin shook her head. "It's pretty fuzzy. I remember going for walks with my dad. He'd take me out, and we'd skip rocks... collect pinecones..."

"You don't remember doing anything with your mom?"

"Maybe playing with dolls once... She probably worked. I was probably at daycare or school during the day and only saw her for a couple of hours during the day."

Charley raised her eyebrows. "I can remember doing things with my mom at that age, and she was a schoolteacher, so she worked all day and then marked papers or prepared lessons in the evening after I went to bed. But I still remember playing with her and cooking supper together."

"There's a lot of stuff from around that time that I don't remember. With the car accident and losing both of my parents, it was a traumatic time." Erin knew she shouldn't have to feel defensive about not remembering much about her mother or their spending time together, but she couldn't help it. She wanted to be able to remember more about her parents. She had tried. "I just wondered what yours were like," Erin said, trying to bring the conversation back to Charley. "What it was like growing up around here. I mostly grew up in the north, you know."

Charley paused in her cookie-arranging. "I think it was a good place to grow up. I loved my mom and dad. We had a nice family. I always wanted brothers and sisters, but I understood they couldn't have them naturally and that it's just not that easy to adopt. They didn't have any involvement with any of the clans, it was just a normal upbringing."

"So…" Erin trailed off, not sure how to ask the question in her mind.

Charley held her gaze, not looking back down at her tray. "So, what happened to me?" she asked. "Why did I turn out like I did?"

Erin shrugged. "I guess. I just wondered…"

"Plenty of kids raised in good homes end up in trouble," Charley said with a shrug. "It doesn't mean there's anything wrong with their parents or with the way they were raised. It just means they… went off the rails. It can happen to anyone. I didn't really like being the good girl. I didn't enjoy all of those things that I was supposed to… going to school, getting good marks, finding a good job and growing up to be a conservative, responsible person. I wanted something more interesting. Something more exciting. I'm sorry, but being good isn't always a whole lot of fun."

Erin gave a little laugh of disbelief and shook her head. "That just sounds so…"

"Silly? I suppose so. Here I am, great upbringing, middle class home, no problems with abuse or drugs or parents who didn't give me enough time. Maybe some of it is nature. I gather that our folks weren't exactly the salt-of-the-earth types. Maybe the Plaint blood is a little more… adventure-seeking."

"I don't know… the ones that I met turned out to be pretty nasty to each other. There was a lot of dysfunction in that family."

"But maybe you can't just blame it all on how their parents raised them. Maybe some of it is just genetic. I have a genetic predisposition to… be an adventure-seeking free spirit. Not to be tied down by convention. Not everyone does want to settle down and raise a family and be responsible parents."

Erin looked away from Charley, readjusting the arrangement of her tray. "And what about you? You don't ever want to raise a family?"

"I think that what's more important to you is 'do I want to settle down and be a business owner?'" Charley pointed out.

"Yeah, I guess. I thought you'd already decided that."

"I did. But it's not easy. And I'm really more of a take-the-easy-way-out person."

"You've hardly even started. You're not considering giving it up already, are you?"

"No. I'm going to stick it out. You can't just give up after a few days. Not when it's taken months to actually get here."

Erin nodded. "Okay. Good. And if you do want out… you'll give me some warning, right? We'd need to find someone to buy you out, and I can't do that right now. I don't know who in Bald Eagle Falls could, but we'd have to try to work something out."

Charley made a motion to brush the topic aside. "Don't worry about it. I'm not taking off any time in the near future."

"Okay." But the talk about the Plaint family made Erin uneasy. Each of the family members that she had dealt with had been unpredictable and left the rest of the family in the lurch. Not of their own free will, but each of their exits had been abrupt and had left some significant ripples.

"We'd better get these out," Charley said. She picked up her tray and took it out to the front of the store. Erin silently followed with her tray and returned to the kitchen to grab the urn of tea and to fill a couple of teapots with boiling water as the first of the church ladies entered the front door, their entrance marked by the friendly jingling of bells.

# Chapter Seven

ERIN WAS SURPRISED TO have Rohilda Beavan show up at the ladies' tea. She hadn't talked to Beaver about it, though she supposed she had probably mentioned it in passing. She hadn't thought that Beaver was a churchgoer, and generally those who didn't attend church weekly didn't go to the ladies' tea, though of course, there was no rule to stop them from doing so.

Beaver's presence was definitely noticed by the regulars, who watched her awkwardly and didn't quite know how to respond to her wide smile, lazy drawl, and constant gum chewing. Moreover, Beaver was dressed as she usually was, in camouflage cargo pants, a tank top, and a hunting jacket, while the usual attire for the women at the ladies' tea was a conservative dress, with only the occasional pantsuit. Erin and Charley were wearing slacks, but the church ladies were all in dresses.

Erin could see that Mary Lou was making an effort to include Beaver and make her feel at home, which Erin appreciated. Mary Lou had found herself on the outside of the group for several months and perhaps that ostracism had made her more sensitive to others around her who didn't quite fit in or look or act the way that they were expected to.

"So… Rohilda… have you moved into Bald Eagle Falls?" Mary Lou inquired, taking a sip of her tea. She did not have any of the sweet treats. She never did. Erin admired her willpower in being able to turn them down.

"No," Beaver responded, leaning her chair back onto two legs, her own legs spread wide, taking up lots of space. "Not full time, anyway, just visiting with Jeremy."

"It's good that he managed to find a place of his own. He seems like a very nice boy." Mary Lou glanced at Erin as if weighing her words and left whatever other comment she had about Jeremy unsaid. Maybe a dig about Jeremy being normal, unlike Vic. Mary Lou had never quite been able to accept Vic's gender identity, though she and Vic had come to an understanding on the matter. Mary Lou would keep her religious opinions about the rightness or wrongness of Vic's identity to herself so that she and Vic and Erin could at least be polite acquaintances, if not friends. In the months since Mary Lou's husband had gone away, Mary Lou had discovered that her good friends from church were not nearly as supportive as she would have expected them to be, and her friendship with Erin and Vic had become more important.

"He's great," Beaver gave Mary Lou a wide smile. "A lot of guys feel threatened by me, but he's very accepting."

"You're quite a bit older than Jeremy, aren't you?" Clara Jones asked, leaning forward and inserting herself into the conversation.

"A bit," Beaver agreed. "Doesn't seem to bother him any." She winked at Clara.

Clara gave a little gasp of shock. Erin tried to suppress a smile, not looking at Charley.

Beaver chewed her gum and looked back at Mary Lou, her eyes dancing.

"And how are your boys?"

Mary Lou gave a restrained smile. "Josh made the basketball team, so he's quite happy about that."

"And how is Cam doing?"

Conversations around them ceased, the other ladies darting curious looks at Mary Lou and Beaver. Erin realized she'd never heard Mary Lou's older son ever called anything but Campbell. Not only that, but he had been living out of town since before Beaver had shown up.

Mary Lou looked at Beaver, her lips pressed together tightly. "Campbell is fine, I suppose. Not that he tells his mother very much."

"Boys." Beaver rolled her eyes in sympathy.

"Do you… know Campbell?"

Beaver shrugged. "We've met."

And Beaver was a federal agent involved in drug enforcement and had done undercover work. Erin could see these facts flash through Mary Lou's mind as she tried to decide whether that meant her son was in trouble.

Beaver's merry eyes went momentarily serious. "He's okay," she told Mary Lou.

Mary Lou touched Beaver's arm. "You're sure?"

Beaver nodded. "Would I lie to a mom?"

Mary Lou's gaze was intense. "Yes, I believe you would."

"Okay, maybe I would," Beaver agreed with a laugh. "But I'm not. He was just fine last I saw."

Mary Lou sipped her tea. Beaver looked away from her, glancing around at the other ladies who had been listening in on the conversation.

"I hear there's some kind of fall fair coming up. What y'all doin' for that?"

They were clearly reluctant to change the subject, wanting to eavesdrop more on what was going on with Mary Lou and her family, but they were too polite to be that obvious about it. So, they turned to describe what crafts, baking, or other items they were preparing for the Fall Fair.

"What about you?" Beaver asked Erin. "You must be planning something special."

# APPLE-ACHIAN TREASURE

Erin nodded. "I don't want to say too much about it yet, I want it to be a surprise. But it is a traditional Tennessean dessert, and Vic is helping me out with all of the details to make sure that all of the usual rules are complied with, even though it will be gluten-free."

Beaver raised her eyebrows and took another cookie off of the platter closest to her. "I gotta say, I haven't ever tasted gluten-free like this before. Are you sure you're not just trying to pull one over on us all?"

"They're gluten-free!" Erin assured her. "Cross my heart!"

"We'd know if they weren't," Clara Jones offered. "Little Peter Foster, for one, wouldn't be able to eat them. He'd be sicker than a dog if Erin was trying to pull something off as gluten-free when it wasn't. And there are a few other people around town who need to eat gluten-free who could tell you they are."

Beaver grinned, nodding. Erin didn't get the feeling that she doubted at all that the treats were gluten-free. She was just being polite and encouraging conversation.

"Well then, I'm looking forward to whatever it is you and Vic are going to pull together for the Fall Fair. It sounds like it's going to be a lot of fun."

"You'll be there, then?" Lottie Sturm asked.

"I expect to be. Of course, work can always throw a wrench into the works. It isn't like I haven't ever had a day off get rescheduled before. But if I can, I'll be there."

"Is Jeremy doing anything for it?"

"I imagine he'll participate in some of the animal handling. He hasn't said yet what he's going to do."

"What about you?" Erin asked. "Are you going to do something?"

"Well, y'all don't want to taste my cooking. So, I won't be submitting any baking or preserves. Maybe I'll go out for the shooting. I'm not bad with a gun."

She patted her waist. Erin swallowed, unnerved by the fact that Beaver carried a gun with her so casually. People didn't attend the ladies' tea wearing guns. It just wasn't done. Something about it being on a Sunday made Erin think that Beaver should have just left her gun at home, even though Erin herself was an atheist. It just didn't seem like it was right for Beaver to bring a gun to the after-church tea.

When Terry dropped by toward the end of the tea, Erin knew that he would be wearing his gun, but somehow that was different. Terry was a police officer in uniform. And a man. Erin apparently had some hitherto unrecognized sexist viewpoints when it came to women wearing guns.

"We've had women win the sharpshooter contests before," Mary Lou commented. "It wouldn't be unheard of if you beat out all the men."

Beaver nodded at this, chewing her gum. "That'd be sweet. I wouldn't mind that at all."

The conversation seemed to have gone back to normal topics. Erin went around with the teapot to refresh anyone's drinks, listening to the casual gossip about what was going on in town.

Nothing to do with her this time. No murders or other mysteries to be solved. As far as everyone was concerned, everything was back to normal. It didn't matter that Auntie Clem's Bakery had moved across the street or that Charley was there helping out now that she was part owner. Everyone seemed completely comfortable with the way things were.

Erin didn't bring up her new mystery. She wasn't about to have the whole town searching for her treasure. Or even worse, spoiling her hunt by telling her that the treasure had been discovered long ago or that it didn't really exist.

She intended to have a good time finding that out for herself.

## Chapter Eight

AT THE END OF the tea, Terry did show up with K9 at his heel to help tidy up, snitch a couple of leftover cookies, and offer to take Erin out for the afternoon. Erin sighed as she gathered teacups to be washed.

"I'd love to go somewhere… but I think I'm going to need to go into town to run a few errands. We did run into a few things that we need to buy for the bakery that we hadn't thought about before. We made do without, but it's easier when you have everything you need."

"How long is that going to take? Maybe we could go into the city together and catch a movie when you're done?"

"I just don't think I'll have time," Erin said reluctantly. "Once I get things done… it would be too late for a matinee, and that means it would be in the evening, and I'd be late getting back and wouldn't be in on time. I just don't think it's going to work this week."

Terry nodded slowly. He looked down at K9 instead of at Erin. "Seems like you've been pretty busy all the time lately. Should I be taking the hint?"

"No," Erin insisted. "No, it's not that at all. I'm not trying to put you off. I have been extra busy, but that's just because of reopening the bakery. After a couple of weeks, it should settle back down to normal again. Then we'll be able to do something."

"You're sure? It's better if you are open about it and just come out and say so if you don't want to see each other anymore."

"I do. I do. I'm not trying to avoid you or push you away. It's just a lot of work. You don't want to come into the city and hold my bag while I shop, do you?"

Terry made a face. "Not my favorite thing to do."

"Then don't worry about it. Things will settle down again and go back to normal."

"And then it will be the Fall Fair. And then you'll be thinking about Halloween and Thanksgiving…"

"Thinking about Halloween and Thanksgiving didn't stop me from spending time with you last year. We just have to fit each other in where we can. Sometimes you're on shift, and sometimes I'm busy with bakery stuff. It will work out if we both want it to."

"As long as you do."

"I do."

"Okay." Terry picked up another cookie. "But I need sugar to comfort myself."

Erin laughed and motioned to the plate. "Take as many as you like. I'm just going to toss them out."

"That would be a waste of good cookies," Terry said through a mouthful, and grabbed two more off of the platter.

K9 looked up at Terry and whined at him.

"K9 wants his too. Come here, K9, come and get one." Erin called K9 over to the cookie jar.

He looked at Terry, and when Terry signaled to him, he trotted over to Erin eagerly to get his treat too. They both munched on their cookies while Erin and Charley carried dishes back to the kitchen to be washed.

Eventually, Erin brushed off her hands. "Okay. That's it for me. I'll see you tomorrow."

Charley looked at her. "I wasn't planning on coming in tomorrow."

# APPLE-ACHIAN TREASURE

"Didn't you sign up for the early shift?" Erin teased.

Charley shook her head adamantly. "I've come to the conclusion that the only way for me to make the early shift would be to stay up and do it before going to bed. There's no way I can get up that early."

"People do it all over the world."

"They're not me. You ask my mom; I was always impossible to get out of bed in the morning. My body just isn't made for mornings."

Erin and Vic hadn't made any plans to see each other in the city, but Erin looked up from her shopping at the kitchen supply store to see a familiar blond head going down the next aisle over. She studied the girl for a moment to make sure she was right, then called out to her.

"Victoriaaaa…"

Vic's head snapped around. She saw Erin and her jaw dropped. She started laughing. "Erin! Aren't you supposed to be taking it easy this afternoon?"

"And I thought you were supposed to be out with Willie."

"I am. Willie?" Vic looked around. "He's around here somewhere. I must have lost him back in appliances. He was looking at something he thought he could use…"

"What are you doing here?"

"We just came out to eat, and I thought that since I was right here, I'd pop in and pick up a few of the things that we needed, and then I'd just text you and let you know that I got them so that we wouldn't both buy the same things. I thought I could save us some time. But you came anyway. I told you to rest this afternoon."

"I couldn't rest, knowing that I still needed to get things for the bakery. I have all of my lists, and today was the only day I was free to run errands. Otherwise, I'd have to wait until next week…"

Vic shook her head. "You're a workaholic. Where's Charley? I bet she's not out taking care of business today. She's out looking after number one, right?"

"She came to the ladies' tea today. But, no, I don't think she's doing anything else today. I think she was taking the rest of the day off."

"And you should have too."

"Said the pot to the kettle."

Willie came around the end of the aisle looking for Vic and put his hands on his hips. "I wasn't told this was an official meeting."

"It's not!" Erin insisted. "It was just chance that we both ended up here. We both thought we could save the other some time. And here we are."

"Using twice as much manpower instead of half," Willie observed. "Well, make quick work of it. Get what it is you need, and then I'll take both of you out to dinner."

"You can take Vic. No need to take me. I'm going to run a few other errands and head back to Bald Eagle Falls."

"Not without supper, you're not. You're here, so you're having supper with us, young lady."

"It's your date night. I'm not going to interfere."

"It's not interfering if you're invited. Now get what you need." He made a hurry-up motion with his hands. "Skedaddle. The faster you get done, the sooner you can have dinner and be on your way. We won't stop anywhere too formal. It will be quick. But you need to eat, so don't argue with me."

Erin shrugged widely and shook her head. She and Vic quickly divvied up the list of supplies they needed to get and went in opposite directions, gathering them up and meeting up again at the till. Willie was standing at the front of the store waiting for them when he was done, with a shopping bag of his own.

## APPLE-ACHIAN TREASURE

"Good. Now there's a pub just down the end there that serves the best wings you ever had. Quick and easy. How about it?"

"I'm yours," Erin said, giving in. He wasn't going to let her back out graciously, so she might as well eat. As he said, she was going to have to anyway.

Once they were settled, Willie tore into his first wing and narrowed his eyes at Erin.

"So, when are you going to tell me about this treasure hunt of yours?"

"Oh…" Erin looked at Vic, surprised. "Well, I didn't really want to bother you. Vic said you were pretty busy with other stuff, so…"

"I want to hear about it. Don't listen to Vic. You know how she is."

Vic laughed. "Does that mean you're offering your services to Erin for free?" she asked. "Because I think we'd better be up front about the arrangements. Do you want to hear, or do you want her to hire you?"

"I want to hear," Willie said. "No charge. If I can think of any way to help, I will. I'm not that miserly."

"I didn't say *miserly*," Vic returned. "I said careful with his money."

Willie made a face at her, then turned his attention back to Erin. "There is a poem? I don't suppose you have it on you?"

"I can remember it," Erin advised. She closed her eyes and envisioned the paper, then recited it to him. Willie thought about it, pursing his lips.

"Interesting. Not a lot of clues in there. At least, not at first. But there may be more than you think. What have you thought of so far?"

"Well… we might be supposed to start at a place that has something to do with a king. Something that has the name of a king or president, or maybe somewhere that looks like a castle or is named after one." Erin looked at Vic. "Right?"

Vic nodded vigorously. "That's where Beaver said to start."

"Good thinking. Well, there are a few places that might fit the bill. We have a rock formation locally known as the turret, because it looks like a castle turret. We have a King's Creek. There is no end of places that could be named after kings like James or Richard. As well as anyplace named after dead presidents. Because they are the kings of the United States."

Erin nodded. "Yeah. I was looking at a map, and there are a lot of places… but I don't really know where to start. I can see them on a map, but I don't know how big an area is covered or how to narrow it down to something searchable. Searching all of King's Creek or James's Forge… I don't know. Is there anywhere that really jumps out at you?"

"We have to look at the rest of the poem for other clues to narrow it down. It has to be somewhere underground, because of the reference to moles."

Erin's stomach gave that familiar nauseated turn at the thought of searching for anything in underground tunnels. "But that doesn't mean that the treasure is in a tunnel. It could just be a clue to something close. Or it could just mean that it's buried, not that it's in a tunnel."

"I'm thinking it means a tunnel," Willie said firmly. "I can't think of any other way that it could be in a mole's burrow. But that doesn't narrow things down a lot, because the number of caves and tunnels in Tennessee outweighs the number of caves in any other state. If you want caves, this is the place to be. But I don't know whether it is a manmade tunnel or a natural cave. I'm thinking manmade, since it talks about toil."

"You don't think that just relates to the crops that the gold was supposed to be payment for?"

"It could be. But you have to look at everything in the poem as having a double meaning. One that is obvious, and one that could mean something else. It has to be understood on more than one level."

"Okay. Maybe a manmade tunnel. And something to do with a king."

"King Solomon's mines?" Vic suggested. "Isn't that a thing? I think there's a movie."

"There is," Willie agreed. "It's from a book. But the book postdates the poem, so I don't think that's what they're referring to."

"But King Solomon goes back to ancient times, doesn't he?" Erin asked. "Isn't he a Bible guy?"

"He is a Bible guy. I don't know if there really is a legend about King Solomon's mines, but if there is… according to the movie, they were in Africa, not Tennessee. I don't think you want to be traveling all the way to the dark continent to try to find this treasure, do you?"

"No," Erin agreed, her face getting warm. "But it could still be a clue. What if there is a Solomon's Creek or Bible Bog?"

Willie nodded his agreement. "Sure. You'll have to see what you can find on the map. But remember that you're looking for something that existed a hundred and fifty years ago, not a new development. You might need to order some old maps to be able to figure it out. It could be somewhere that doesn't exist anymore too. It might be a ghost town or a farm that changed its name a hundred years ago. Survey maps are probably the best bet, they'll refer to local landmarks of the time as much as possible. I have a few that I could lend you."

"You don't know of a King Solomon river, do you?"

"No. Nothing that pops to mind."

"How about the rest of it? Any ideas as to what the other clues might be?"

"Did you find anything in the newspapers of the time? Anything that was happening in the area at the time?"

"Mostly war stuff, births, deaths, marriages… there wasn't really a lot of real news. So-and-so's barn burned down. There was a big cucumber crop. I don't know. Nothing that seems like it would have much significance."

"Have you gone to the library archives or just looked through Clementine's files with Vic?"

Erin looked over at Vic, seeing that she had already told Willie all about the evening they had spent looking for clues in the dusty file. "So far, just Clementine's files. I'm not even sure how far back the library will be able to go."

"If they don't have anything, some of the bigger libraries in the capital might have something. I know some of them have archives that go back that far. Don't know how much local color they'd have. Might not be helpful at all."

Erin nodded. "Okay."

"Remember that if Clementine had all of the information in her files, she probably would have figured it out herself. The fact that she never figured out that there really was a treasure or where it might have been suggests that she never had the full story. She just had the poem, and didn't have enough background to make it into anything meaningful."

"I guess that makes sense." Erin had been wondering whether she would need to look through all of Clementine's other files and genealogy books to find more clues, but Willie was probably right. If Clementine had had all of the clues, there wouldn't have been a mystery.

"So, I'll need to go to the library. And you have some maps that I could look at that might be better than Google maps?"

"Google maps has its place, especially if you can spot changes in terrain from digging, but it isn't as likely to give you those historical names. We'll need to work on the assumption that whoever wrote that poem lived around here and would have had limited transportation abilities."

"How limited?"

"Horse and wagon. A king's ransom of gold is too heavy for a man to carry. Limiting it to… say three days' wagon ride?"

"Which is?" Vic prompted.

"Maybe sixty miles."

It was still a pretty fair distance, but not so daunting as having to consider all of Tennessee.

# Chapter Nine

ERIN HAD TOLD TERRY that she would be able to keep the treasure hunt a secret, shared with only their few close friends, but rumors spread much more quickly than she ever would have predicted. Searching through newspaper archives at the library attracted a certain amount of attention, even when Erin said it was for genealogy. Everyone she saw there wanted to know what genealogical line she was working on and who she was looking for. With all of the shared kinship in Bald Eagle Falls, everyone was related to everyone else, and anyone who was interested probably knew the genealogy of the whole mountain. Going back a hundred and fifty years was nothing; everybody seemed to know their family trees at least that far back. Many of them from memory.

As much as Erin tried to bluff her way through the conversations, it soon became obvious to people that she had something to hide, and the attempts to discover what she was working on became more and more of a problem. Erin neglected to close her clipboard one day, and the eagle-eyed librarian seemed to have read the poem from all the way across the room.

"Is that what you're up to?" Betty Thompson demanded. "You think there's a buried treasure?"

"I don't know," Erin said, trying to brush it off. "It's just a poem. I haven't found anything in the archives that would back it up."

## APPLE-ACHIAN TREASURE

"There have always been rumors of treasures hidden in these parts. If we knew which one the poem is talking about…"

"I'm not sure. I'll need to do some more research."

Betty was staring at Erin's clipboard, even though she had closed it when Betty approached, and Erin knew by the look in her eye that she was reconstructing it and visualizing it in her mind's eye. Betty Thompson's photographic memory was a legend in Bald Eagle Falls and made her a fantastic resource as a librarian. If she saw something once, she would remember it, and when you were looking for it again, she could pinpoint it in seconds. Faster than a Google search on a super computer.

"The paper and the script would suggest wartime," she said slowly, "so they're not talking pirate gold or early colonial days. More likely gold payroll. Preserving life could be referring to armies or soldiers. Not being forced to serve could refer to slavery."

Erin blinked at her. "Wow. You really are good. I don't know how you even saw that."

"All I need is one look, my dear! You know who is really good with civil war history? Edna, come over here!"

Erin tried to protest, holding up her hand to stop Betty, but Betty talked right over her protests, inviting Edna, a white-haired woman a few tables away, to come over to ask for her insights. Edna came over to them, and Erin again tried to politely wave them off.

"No, really, it's okay, I just wanted to work on this by myself—"

"Nonsense," Betty said jovially, "the more people who can help, the better chance you'll have of solving this. Now let's have a look…"

In spite of Erin's attempt to keep the poem out of sight, Betty quickly slid the clipboard out from under Erin's hand and opened it up to show to Edna. Erin was loath to kick up a big fuss in the middle of the library, attracting even more attention to her treasure hunt. She sat there with her mouth open, trying to think of what to say to dissuade them from their course.

The two women read over the poem again and discussed what the various lines of the poem might refer to. Erin couldn't help getting drawn into the conversation and gave in to listening to their insights and asking more detailed questions about the history of the area and the way that payment, and gold in particular, would have been handled a hundred and fifty years before.

Edna was definitely an expert on the matter, sketching out a rough map for Erin and pointing out the different routes that would have been used for transporting crops to market and gold back home, identifying the various landmarks along the way, and suggesting where a delivery might be lost or hijacked along the way.

"Wow, this is more than I ever could have gotten from a newspaper article," Erin said, amazed at the deep knowledge Edna and Betty had, "I didn't even know where to start."

"I would say that you need to look for mines and caves in this general area," Edna said, tapping her finger on the hand-drawn map. "It's close enough that someone in Bald Eagle Falls could have run into the wagon, but far enough away that the other residents would never know that the delivery had come so close. There are a few old mines around there. One person or a small group of people would have to be able to get the gold from the wagon to the hiding place, and gold is heavy, so they wouldn't be able to move it far. It's rough going out there in the wilds. It wasn't a highway like we're used to now. Just a rough track, and moving the treasure out of the wagon into a cave or mine would have been even rougher, cutting through brush and moving over uneven ground."

Erin nodded. "I know someone who might have some maps of the area and could help me out."

## APPLE-ACHIAN TREASURE

The women exchanged glances with each other.

"Willie Andrews," Betty asked.

Erin shouldn't have been shocked. Everybody in Bald Eagle Falls knew everybody else's business, and of course they would know that Erin knew Willie and that he was involved in mining and other ventures and would have all kinds of maps of the area. But she hadn't been expecting them to make that connection quite so quickly.

"Uh…"

They smiled at each other, as if she were some cute two-year-old who didn't understand the ways of adults.

"I really don't want this spread around," Erin hoped to mitigate some of the damage. "Do you think you could keep quiet about it? I don't want other people joining in the search… you know…"

"Of course not," Betty agreed. "This is your little treasure hunt, and good luck to you! We're not going to spread it around to all of our friends."

But Erin had a sinking feeling that each of them would tell at least one other person. And two more people aware of the hunt became four more people, and it wouldn't be long before everyone in Bald Eagle Falls had heard about Erin's possible hidden gold and were on the hunt for it as well.

Meanwhile, life went on at Auntie Clem's Bakery. Erin worked long hours and there was always plenty to do, not leaving her a lot of time for treasure hunting. She also had the Fall Fair to prepare for.

Vic sat down beside Erin to show her the recipes that she had gathered.

"So, this is how a Tennessee stack cake is made. It's not like any other layer cake you ever made. It's not all light and fluffy and loads of icing."

Erin skimmed the recipes for the pertinent details, frowning. "No… this is very different…"

"The layers are real thin," Vic explained. "You bake them like cookies, not like cakes, so that they're kind of hard and dry. They're dark and spicy, like gingerbread cookies."

"Okay."

"And you make the apple sauce. It's not applesauce like you buy in a jar at the store. You have to make it out of dried apples, and it's real thick and flavorful."

"And then you layer them."

"Right. A layer of cake, and then a thick layer of the apple filling. You have to have at least six layers for a genuine stack cake, and some of them are as high as fifteen layers. That's a sky-high stack cake."

"And the apple filling is supposed to soak into the layers of cake."

"You have to wrap it up real tight and let it sit for a full day. Better if it's three, but never less than one. The moisture from the apple filling gets into the cake and makes it real moist and rich."

"I've never heard of anything like that before."

"People who lived in these parts had lean times. They had to figure out ways to preserve food and then use it. No one wants to just eat dried apples all day. You make yourself a stack cake, and you've got another way to use that apple harvest. It's so good."

"And it should work well as a gluten-free recipe," Erin mused. "Since it's not something that's light and fluffy and has an open structure like angel food cake, you don't need to rely on gluten to help it to rise and hold its shape. It's okay if it's flat."

"It's supposed to be flat."

"And the lack of gluten will keep it nice and tender. It won't get rubbery like when you over-mix a wheat flour muffin batter. And the apple sauce will keep it from being dry and crumbly."

## APPLE-ACHIAN TREASURE

Vic nodded. She was getting more familiar with how gluten worked in baking and how to adjust for its lack. "That's one of the reasons I thought of stack cake."

"Brilliant. And we'll add our own twist, something just a little different that will combine the old and the new…"

"You're not already doing that by making it gluten-free?"

"No. I don't want them to be able to tell it is gluten-free. But I do want to give it something extra to give it a little update."

They were in the kitchen cleaning up when Vic's phone rang. Since they had already closed up shop, she stopped and took it out of her apron pocket. Her forehead creased in a frown, and she tapped the screen to answer it.

"Hello? Yes?"

Erin saw Vic's face rapidly lose all color. She hurried to Vic's side to catch her by the arm before she could faint.

"Vicky? What is it? What happened?"

Vic lowered the phone from her ear, staring at Erin, her eyes wide. "It's Jeremy."

"What happened?"

"He's been shot."

Erin's hand tightened on Vic's arm. She shook her head slightly, not believing it.

"What? How did he get shot?" Her mind went immediately to Beaver and her gun. Why hadn't she protected him? Or had Beaver been the one who had shot him? Had they had a lover's quarrel? Had they been target shooting and hadn't been careful enough?

Or had it been the Jackson clan?

What could possibly have happened?

"I don't know. They've taken him to the hospital. In the city. I have to go. Can I use your car?"

Erin took a quick look around the kitchen. All of the ovens were turned off and all of the batters and doughs were in the fridge. "We can leave the rest. I'll drive you."

"I can drive myself. You can get Terry to pick you up or you can walk home."

"I'm not letting you drive after having news like that. And I want to be there at the hospital, not at home waiting to find out what happened."

"You don't have to come."

"I know that. I want to. He's my friend."

Vic swallowed and gave a quick nod. "Okay. Thanks. You're sure we can leave everything?"

"It's just dirty, nothing is going to go bad. We'll take care of it later."

Vic headed for the back door. Erin shut off the lights and locked the door behind them.

## Chapter Ten

IT SEEMED LIKE IT took forever to get to the hospital. As Erin drove, she remembered Willie driving her when she had been poisoned. He'd grabbed Terry's police vehicle and sped all the way there. Erin wished that she had lights and a siren or a police escort, but she didn't and that meant that she couldn't speed all the way there. It just wasn't safe. She pressed the gas as far as she dared, not wanting to get pulled over and to have to explain to a policeman why they were going so fast.

Vic's hands were in her lap, her long, white fingers twisting together in her anxiety to get there and find out what had happened.

"I'm going as fast as I dare," Erin told her.

"I know. It's okay. We'll get there. I'm sure it's nothing. He probably shot himself in his foot loading his gun." She gave a little laugh that ended up sounding like a squeak or a hiccup.

"Yes. It's probably nothing," Erin agreed. But she didn't think it was nothing. If it was nothing, then Jeremy himself would have called Vic instead of the hospital. He would have laughed and made a big joke out of it, like he did about everything.

Finally, they were into the city, and Erin navigated the streets, keeping an eye out for the 'H' street signs indicating the route to the hospital. She hadn't been there enough times to know the way without them. She pulled up to the emergency doors.

"You go ahead. I'll go find parking and see you in a few minutes."

"Thanks, Erin." Vic jumped out, slammed the door behind her, and dashed in through the doors.

Parking was always an issue at the hospital; space was at a premium and they charged an arm and a leg for it. Erin laughed grimly at the thought of a hospital charging and arm and a leg, but she knew it wasn't really very funny. She was just anxious.

She had to work her way through the maze of hallways from the parking structure, following cryptic signs and ending up in the wrong wing more than once. Finally, she made it back to emergency after going out of the hospital and walking around the outside to the doors she had dropped Vic at.

She looked around the groups of chairs for Vic. She wasn't there, but was standing near the triage desk looking lost.

"What is it?" Erin asked, the pulse in her throat pounding so hard she could hardly hear. "What did you find out?"

"He's in surgery. He got shot in the torso, they won't say how bad it is."

"How did he get shot?"

"I don't know yet. They said someone would come out to talk to me. There are police…" She looked over her shoulder to the area behind the security glass where doctors and nurses were busy with their usual activities. There were several dark-uniformed cops in close conversation with each other. As Erin watched, one of them broke away from the group and swiped his card to open the security door that got him back into the waiting area. He nodded at Vic.

"You're Jeremy's sister?"

## APPLE-ACHIAN TREASURE

Vic nodded. "Yes. What happened? Is he going to be okay?"

"We still need to finish taking statements." He motioned them toward the grouping of chairs close by.

Erin guided Vic over to one of them and sat down beside her, keeping a comforting hand on her shoulder. The policeman remained on his feet.

"As I say, we're still investigating, but the bottom line is that he was shot at work, exchanging gunfire with a poacher."

"At work?" Vic echoed. She shook her head. "How does he get in a gunfight with a poacher in broad daylight?"

"The farm has had issues with poaching, which is why your brother was hired. We'll have to have some discussions about whether everyone was properly licensed and registered. As you say, it was pretty bold, planning a daylight robbery, but that appears to be what happened."

Vic rubbed her hand across her eyes and forehead. "What are they growing that is so valuable? Please tell me it's not drugs. Are they growing marijuana or poppies?"

He gave a sympathetic smile. "Everything appears to be legal."

"Well, thank goodness for that."

Erin noted that the officer still hadn't disclosed what it was that they were growing.

Time passed slowly. Erin sat and rubbed Vic's back and they spoke quietly to each other in fits and starts, mostly sitting silently, but occasionally talking about something unimportant as it came to mind. Erin watched the clock on the wall, as she was sure Vic did, willing the time to pass faster and for Jeremy to be out of surgery, fully restored.

After a couple of hours, Vic looked up, her eyes tired and swollen.

"Your knight in shining armor has arrived," she observed.

Erin followed Vic's gaze and saw Terry approaching with K9 at his side. He spotted the two of them and moved with more certainty.

"Vic. How is he? Do you know anything?"

"No, not yet. He's in surgery. Took a bullet somewhere in his body. That's all we know. Just… waiting for word of how the surgery goes."

Terry shook his head. He pulled a chair over, scraping the floor noisily. "I can't believe it. I figured he'd get in trouble while he was with the Jackson clan, or trying to get out of it, not when he got a legitimate job."

"It is legitimate, right?" Vic asked.

"As far as I can tell. I'm not getting any chatter that there's anything illegal going on. It seems to be all aboveboard."

"I can't believe it either. He's a good shot, so how did this poacher get the drop on him?"

"It sounds like there was more than one of them. So, he might have been pincered between two of them. I can't imagine that they'd be intentionally approaching him rather than trying to get… whatever it was they were trying to get, but there's no telling. Maybe he snuck up on one and didn't see the lookout."

"Did he get any of them?"

"We think so. They got away, but there is enough blood at the scene that he probably got at least one of them. We don't know how badly or how far they'll be able to travel. It will take time to do all of the blood analysis, of course; we're just going from droplet patterns at this point. They'll do typing and maybe DNA to sort it all out. If they think it's important. It might not really matter."

"Why wouldn't they?" Erin demanded. "They'd want to track down and arrest whoever these poachers are, wouldn't they? Why wouldn't they follow up on every lead?"

"Because testing takes time and money that could be better spent on other things. A couple of poachers don't rank high on the priorities list. Not when you've got drugs, gangs, and murders to deal with. Nothing was actually stolen, so there are no losses. It's just Jeremy's injury. Weapons and assault charges. And more than likely, they'll catch these guys when they show up somewhere for medical care. No need to waste money on unnecessary testing."

"It isn't important that Jeremy got injured?" Erin asked in disbelief.

"Not in the grand scheme of things, no." Terry looked away uncomfortably. "That doesn't mean that I don't care, it just means that's the way they prioritize resources. Of course, I care that Jeremy got hurt. I'm here. I want to support Vic and to make sure he's okay. It's not 'nothing' to me. But to bureaucrats who don't know him... it doesn't mean much to them. Just one non-fatal injury."

Vic choked up. Terry reached out to her and Vic held his hand.

"He's going to be okay, Vic," Terry said. "He'll be laughing about this before you know it."

"You don't know that. He could... he could be badly hurt. He could be..."

"Let's not jump to conclusions. I'm sorry. I didn't mean it to sound like that. He's going to be okay."

"If he is, he'd better not go back to this job again," Vic said forcefully. "He can find another job. This is crazy. Who shoots someone over a cornfield? I can't understand it."

"Corn?" Terry repeated.

"I don't know what they're growing. No one has actually said. But the policeman who was here and talked to us said that it wasn't drugs. It wasn't anything illegal. I can't think of what anyone would be growing that was that valuable."

"Maybe some kind of orchid," Erin suggested. "I know there are some really rare species that are really hard to grow. They need special greenhouses and monitoring equipment... maybe it's something like that."

"Maybe it is. I don't know." Vic ground her teeth. "Orchids!"

They were all quiet for a while. Terry looked at Erin.

"Do you want me to take you home? You can leave your car here for Vic."

"No, I'm not going anywhere. We need to know that Jeremy is out of danger."

"Oh, I know. I meant after that. When everything is sorted out and you're ready to go."

Erin shook her head. "No. I'll stay. Thanks."

"Okay…"

Erin looked at him. "What?"

Terry raised his brows questioningly.

"What's that tone?" Erin asked.

"No tone."

Erin looked at Vic for confirmation. "There was a definite tone," she insisted. "So, what is it? What's the problem with me staying here?"

Vic gave a little nod of confirmation, looking at Terry curiously. "There was something."

"No tone," Terry insisted. "I was just thinking that… you seem to have gotten pretty close to Jeremy. It seems strange that you're so protective of him and concerned about him when really, you hardly know him." He paused. "Because you really do barely know him, don't you…?"

Erin blinked. "You're jealous? I'm here because I'm concerned about my best friend and her brother, and you're jealous over that?"

"I just wonder… if it's more than that."

"Oh, good grief!" Erin blew her breath out in exasperation. "I'm not secretly in love with Jeremy. I'm here to support my friend. I care about Jeremy. I can care about someone without being… in a relationship with him."

"Of course you can," he agreed, his voice carefully neutral.

"And I do care about him. But we're not in a relationship. We're just friends. Like you say, we really don't know each other very well. But I know Vic."

He nodded slowly. "He was living in your house."

"I told you that there was nothing going on between us. He had his room and I had mine. I'm at the bakery all day and I just squeeze in a few hours of sleep each night. I don't have time to be running the bakery and going out with you and carrying on a torrid affair with Jeremy on the side."

Vic snorted and started to laugh. "A torrid affair?" she repeated. "Erin and Jeremy?"

Terry's face flushed red. "I never said that. I just worry that… there was more going on than Erin and Jeremy would like to admit. I don't even mean there was anything going on between them physically, but you don't know what people are thinking about… and they were living together, keeping it a secret."

"Because the Jackson clan was after Jeremy. You know exactly why he was living there. And you know that I told you as soon as I could. Before he wanted me to."

"Yeah."

"You think that he didn't want me to tell you because he had designs on me? He was hoping that if he kept it a secret that he was living there that… somehow, he'd get his chance with me? Even though I was still dating you?" Erin shook her head vehemently. "There's no way, Terry! And you know he's with Beaver now, so why you're still worrying about anything…"

Vic frowned and looked around. "Beaver."

Erin looked over at her, the same thought crystallizing in her mind. "Where *is* Beaver? Why isn't she here already? Didn't anyone let her know what was going on? Wouldn't Jeremy have asked them to call her?"

"If he could have," Vic agreed, "but maybe he couldn't."

"He had them call you."

"They called me… but I was his emergency contact at work. He told me that he put my name down because he wasn't sure where things would go with Beaver or if she'd always be available if something happened. You know, if she's undercover, they wouldn't be able to reach her, and she wouldn't be able to reach any of us. They wouldn't know to call me if they couldn't reach her."

"Do you have her number? Maybe no one has contacted her."

Vic shook her head. Erin looked at Terry. "Do you have her number? Or could you get it from someone?"

"I have it," Terry confirmed. He pulled out his phone and turned it on to check the contact phone numbers. Erin looked at Vic while Terry was looking it up.

"Me and Jeremy," she scoffed. "I mean, Jeremy's a nice guy, but I'm in a relationship already. And so is he, now. I love him like a brother. I never looked at him any other way."

"I know that," Vic said, but there was something in her eyes.

Erin frowned, getting a headache from the tension across her forehead. "Not you too? I didn't have romantic feelings toward Jeremy."

"No."

"Are you saying that he has feelings for me?"

Vic took a little too long to answer the question. Erin's heart beat faster. She looked at Terry, who had looked up from his phone and had his eyes fixed on Vic's face.

"He might have had an interest," Vic said carefully. "He wouldn't horn in on another man's girlfriend, so it's not like he would ever do anything about it, but that didn't mean he didn't have feelings."

"But he's with Beaver now."

Vic nodded quickly. "Yes. And they're getting along famously. I'm just saying that I wouldn't be able to say that he never had any feelings toward you."

"I'm older than he is," Erin dismissed.

"So is Beaver."

"Well… yes."

"So maybe he likes older women."

"That's just…" Words failed Erin. She looked back at Terry. "That doesn't mean anything. It doesn't mean there was ever anything between us. Maybe he liked me, I don't know, he never said or did anything inappropriate. We never did anything."

## Chapter Eleven

ERIN WAS SITTING WITH her hands over her eyes, elbows resting on her knees. She was done with talking. Done with trying to figure out how Jeremy could have been shot over some plants. Done with trying to explain to Terry that she wasn't attracted to Jeremy and he wasn't attracted to her and there was no need for concern. She was so done with waiting for the doctors to come out and tell them how Jeremy had fared with his surgery that she was at the end of her rope.

She heard the thud of approaching boots, and didn't look up, knowing that it wasn't going to be the doctor. Not in boots.

"So just what did that boy do now?" Beaver's voice was loud over the muted whispers of the emergency room.

Erin dropped her hands from her eyes and looked at Beaver. "You made it."

"Of course I made it. Now somebody tell me what's going on."

Even though Beaver's body language said she was completely relaxed and her voice was good-humored, Erin was sure she detected something around Beaver's eyes that said that she was just as concerned about his welfare as everyone else who was waiting there.

"We don't know exactly what happened," Erin sighed.

## APPLE-ACHIAN TREASURE

"He was shot at work," Vic explained once more. "Poachers. More than one, according to Terry," Vic nodded to him, and Terry nodded. "They exchanged gunfire. Jeremy was hit somewhere in the body. He's in surgery." Vic pressed a button on her phone to wake up the screen. "He's been in there for two and a half hours."

"He was shot at work? I thought I was the one who was supposed to have the dangerous job. Isn't that what we agreed to?"

Erin couldn't bring herself to laugh at Beaver's humor. Beaver looked at the sad little group. She dragged a chair over.

"If he's been in there for two and a half hours, then they are probably almost done," she said. "The doctor will be out before long, telling us that everything is going to be just fine. Then I'm going to kill him."

"The doctor or Jeremy?" Vic asked.

"Jeremy. Definitely Jeremy. How could he do this to me?"

Vic shook her head. "How could he do this to any of us? He was supposed to be safe. He left the farm and left the clan and he was supposed to be safe now. I wasn't supposed to have to worry about him anymore."

"Either he didn't get the memo, or he didn't understand it," Beaver grumbled.

"I don't know what I'm going to do," Vic said. "If I have to tell my parents that he's…" she gulped. "I just can't do it, Beaver. I can't call them and tell them that something happened to him."

"You're not going to have to. He'll tell them himself when he gets out."

Vic sighed and shook her head, unconvinced. Erin grasped her hand and gave it a squeeze. She didn't have the words to make Vic feel better. All she could do was be there.

"Where's Willie?" she asked.

"He was doing a long courier run. He couldn't get back. He'll turn around as soon as he can and meet us here."

Erin nodded. "He probably won't be long, then."

"No." Vic turned and looked at the entrance. "Shouldn't be too long."

Beaver pulled out her phone and started tapping away on it. Erin was relieved not to have to carry on a conversation again. She just covered her eyes and waited some more. Surely, as Beaver said, it wouldn't be too long before Jeremy was out of surgery and they would have something to tell them. They would say that he'd need some time to recover, but then he'd be just fine.

It was still another hour before a tired-looking woman in scrubs came out and looked around.

"Family of Jeremy?" she asked.

Vic stood up like a shot. Erin and the others got to their feet more slowly.

"How is he? Is he going to be okay?" Vic demanded.

"He's going to be okay," the doctor said. She put her hand on Vic's arm. "Just calm down there, hon'. Take a deep breath."

Vic did so, swaying slightly on her feet.

"Are you the girlfriend or the sister?" the doctor asked.

"Sister."

"He's in recovery now, and he's awake and asking for you. And you," she turned and looked at Beaver. "You must be the girlfriend."

Beaver nodded. "Yep. But I don't know if you actually want to invite me in there right now, because I might just try to knock some sense into that boy."

The doctor gave a little smile. "I don't normally encourage that sort of thing, but I hope this is the last time I'll see him on my table. I know that boy's insides a lot better than anyone should."

## APPLE-ACHIAN TREASURE

"He's really okay?" Vic asked. "Where did he get shot? Where did the bullet go in?"

"He's okay," the doctor confirmed. "He's stable for now, and he's awake and alert. We'll need to keep an eye on him to make sure that he doesn't get an infection and that we patched up all of the appropriate holes, but I think you can expect a full recovery. He seems like a strong boy, so I imagine he'll bounce back from this pretty quickly and be back out there causing trouble again. I'd just appreciate it if you make sure that he doesn't end up on my table again."

"Yeah," Vic said sourly. "We'll work on that."

"He took two bullets to the torso, but he was lucky and everything seems to be clean. No major organs, intestines are intact, it was mostly just muscle and a lot of blood."

"Two bullets." Beaver shook her head. "Well, he's got me beat. I've only ever had one at a time."

The doctor's jaw dropped as she looked at Beaver. Erin waited for Beaver to laugh and say that she was just kidding, but Beaver didn't. She just gave Erin and the others raised eyebrows and a rueful smile.

"How many times have you been shot?" the doctor demanded. "And what exactly is it that you do?"

"If I told you that, I'd have to kill you," Beaver quipped. "Let's just say that my job has certain hazards. I don't plan on getting shot again, if that makes you feel better. It wasn't a whole lot of fun the first time. Or the second, for that matter."

"You're pulling my leg."

"Nope." Beaver hooked a finger into her collar and tugged back her shirt to show off a scar below her collarbone.

The doctor looked closely at it and shook her head. "You might not be the best person to tell Jeremy to stay out of trouble."

"Maybe I *am* the best person to tell him, since I have the most experience in the area. At least, I assume so…"

She looked at Terry, who shook his head, and then at Erin, who shook hers.

"I've never been shot," Erin said. "I *almost* was once, but Vic shot him." She nodded to Vic.

The doctor made a noise of disbelief.

"But you've been *almost* killed the most times of any of us," Vic said. "Unless Terry…"

Terry again shook his head. "I may be a cop, but I've led a pretty charmed life. I've never been in any life-threatening situation. And I plan to keep it that way."

"Good goal to have," the doctor agreed. "Well, I don't want all of you back there, but maybe if sister and girlfriend would like to come and just say hello to him, then we need to let him rest for a while. He'll need a lot of sleep the next few days for his body to recover and start building up strength again. It was quite a shock to his system."

Vic and Beaver followed the doctor out of the waiting room into the area beyond the security glass. Erin sat back down again, letting out her breath in a long stream.

"Okay. I'm beat. That was scary."

Terry nodded. He sat down beside her again and reached over tentatively to massage her shoulders. Erin melted into him, letting the muscles relax under his practiced hands.

"Oh, that feels good. I was so scared."

"We all were," Terry agreed. He didn't sound jealous like he had before. Maybe he had finally gotten it through his head that Erin wasn't scared because she was in love with Jeremy, but just because he was a friend and that he was Vic's brother.

"You won't ever get shot, will you?" Erin demanded. "I've decided I don't like you being a cop. I don't want to ever have to be here waiting to see if you're going to come out okay."

"I can't promise that nothing will ever happen to me, but neither can you. It wasn't that long ago that you were here after being poisoned and we were all sitting around here wondering whether Willie had gotten you here in time."

"Oh…" Erin smiled weakly. "I'd forgotten about that. All of it is sort of a blur, for a few days."

"But you're okay now, and you're not going to get poisoned again, are you?"

"No." Erin was definite about that. "It's not going to happen again. What are the chances that I would get poisoned twice, anyway?"

"I have no idea. But with you… I suspect it's higher than with most of us."

"It's not my fault. I didn't really do anything to attract attention. People just… think that I know things when I don't."

"They'll think it less if you don't ask so many questions."

Erin shrugged. "Well, I'm not asking anything now. We haven't had any murders and I'm not going to upset anyone. That's all over."

"Now you're just hunting treasures."

Erin looked sideways at him. "Well… yeah. But that's not the same. It doesn't belong to anyone. It isn't anyone's secret. It isn't related to anyone dying or poisoning anyone. It's just… something fun to do."

"If you want something fun to do, take up geocaching. Or knitting. Or needlepoint."

"I'm not taking up needlepoint."

"Or knitting," Terry prompted.

"Not knitting, either."

Erin saw Willie looking around at the other people in the waiting room and waved to get his attention. He joined them, looking at Vic's empty chair.

"I gather she's in with him?"

Erin nodded. She relayed the details the doctor had given them. Willie sat down.

"I guess I missed all of the fun stuff. But I can't say I'm disappointed about that. Poor Vic. I'm glad you were here for her."

Erin nodded. "I'm not sure it did any good, but I'm glad too. Hopefully, after this, Jeremy will find something else to do. I don't want anything like this to happen again!"

"I wouldn't have expected it with a job like this," Willie said, shaking his head. "I've heard some pretty interesting things about operations like this, but I don't think violence is high on the list of expectations."

"Operations like this?"

Willie raised his eyebrows and looked back and forth at the two of them. "Well… places that grow valuable plants or raise endangered species. There are always poachers, but you don't usually see violence like this."

"What do you know about this farm that Jeremy's been working on?" Terry asked.

"They're well-known in the business," Willie said slowly. "Good reputation. I haven't heard about them doing anything underhanded. They stick to the rules for harvesting plants, have a good reputation for quality goods. No counterfeit plants."

Erin shook her head. "I've never heard of this kind of thing going on at a farm. What's gotten into people?"

"It isn't common for people to get shot," Willie repeated. "There is theft, yes. There's a reason they hire security, especially during harvest. But believe me, no one could have predicted that this was going to happen to Jeremy."

Erin sighed. "Okay. Got it."

Terry scraped back his chair as he got up. "I don't know about you two, but I'm going to need a coffee if I'm going to stay here much longer. Willie?"

"Love one," Willie agreed.

"Erin?"

## APPLE-ACHIAN TREASURE

Erin shook her head. "Not so close to bedtime, I'll never get to sleep. Something non-caffeinated."

"I'll see what I can find. No Monster energy drinks, then?"

She punched him lightly on the arm. "No Monsters."

Terry and K9 left in search of beverages. Willie gave a deep sigh and leaned back in the chair. Erin knew from experience that there wasn't really any way to get comfortable in the hard plastic chairs. She could see a couple of people who had fallen asleep, but she had no idea how they had managed it. She could only guess that they were very sick. She tried to cover a yawn, but was too tired to repress it. Tears leaked out the corners of her eyes.

"Long day," Willie acknowledged. "You guys are up so early in the morning."

"Yeah. I don't know what I'm going to do tomorrow. I'd call Bella and see if she and Charley could open, but Bella has never prepped by herself, and I'm sure there's no way Charley would be able to get up that early."

"You might just have to open late or be closed for a day."

"I hate to do that."

"Of course. But people will understand. And it isn't like you're providing emergency services. People will survive without their morning muffin."

"I know…"

Willie changed the subject. "How's the treasure hunt coming along?"

Erin was glad to talk about something else, though she wasn't sure she wanted to be talking about treasure hunting when Terry made his way back with their drinks. "Interesting! I learned a lot from Betty and Edna at the library. They really know their stuff."

"They do," Willie agreed. "If you want to know about the history of Bald Eagle Falls, you couldn't ask for much better. But…"

Erin looked at him, frowning. "But what? They're not making it up, are they? They do know what they're talking about."

"They know what they're talking about. It's just that they talk about it an awful lot."

"Meaning…"

"Meaning you may have let the cat out of the bag. Loose lips."

"They said they would keep it quiet. They understood and said they wouldn't talk about it…"

"Uh-huh." Willie's skepticism was clear. "I wouldn't count on it."

All of the effort she had made to keep her treasure hunt quiet, and they were going to spoil it for her. "So I guess I'd better get out ahead of it. Did you find some maps for me?"

Willie looked blank for a moment, as if he'd forgotten all about it. "Yeah, they're in the truck. I can give them to you tonight. You know what you're looking for?"

"I have a better idea." Erin told him about Edna's knowledge about the routes that a payroll wagon probably would have taken. "Do you want to get your maps now? We could look at them together?"

Willie shook his head. "I don't think we need other people seeing us looking at them. Or listening in." He glanced around. "It may look like nobody is listening to us, but I can assure you that's not the case. Half the people here who look like they are sleeping are probably eavesdropping on our conversation. They don't need to see what those routes are that Edna told you about."

Erin looked around at the bored and sleeping people in the waiting room. No one twitched or gave her any sign that they were listening to the conversation between her and Willie. No one smiled to give away the fact that they knew they had been caught. A nurse moved around picking up newspapers, coffee cups, and candy wrappers.

## APPLE-ACHIAN TREASURE

Erin was pretty sure that no one was really listening to them.

# Chapter Twelve

WHEN VIC GOT BACK from seeing Jeremy, she looked exhausted, but there was a light in her features that hadn't been there before she went in to see him. Erin was relieved. She was comforted by the fact that Vic looked peaceful and relaxed instead of more wound up about Jeremy's injuries.

"He's going to sleep now," she told Erin. "He needs his rest. But he really is okay."

"He talked to you?"

"Yeah. He wasn't all loopy, but he was a bit… sedated still. Not quite his usual self, but he was trying. He looked a lot better than I expected him to."

Beaver nodded her agreement. "I'm sure I didn't look anywhere near that good after I got shot," she contributed. "They've given him plenty of blood, so that helps. But he seemed… strong. Like there was no doubt he was on the road to recovery."

Vic smiled. "It's such a relief. When we get home, I'll call Mom and let her know what happened. I didn't earlier because I didn't think there was any point in upsetting them when I didn't know how he was."

"Will they come out and see him?"

Vic shrugged. "I don't know how things are between them. I never really asked. I assume they're not real happy about him leaving home and splitting from the clan, but it

## APPLE-ACHIAN TREASURE

isn't like they kicked him out like with me. I think they're still on speaking terms."

As much as Vic loved her family, they were not prepared to talk with her for as long as she was living a life that was so different from what they had raised her to.

"I love my family," Vic said, echoing what Erin was thinking. "But they can be pretty hardheaded sometimes. Rednecks." She gave a little laugh.

"Are you ready to go home?"

Vic yawned and nodded.

"Are you going with Erin or with me?" Willie asked.

"Oh…" Vic looked form one to the other uncertainly. "I don't know. How are you doing, Erin? Are you okay to drive? Do you need someone to keep you awake?"

"I'm pretty wound up. I don't think keeping awake is going to be a problem."

"Are you sure? I'll go with you if you need someone. I don't want you having an accident on the way home from the hospital."

"I'll be fine. I'll walk out with you, though, Willie has some maps for me."

Erin was sure that whoever had designed the hospital and the parking around it had to have been on drugs at the time. Or maybe none of it was planned and it had just been added on to haphazardly until it was a complete mess that no one could have sorted out. She suspected that even the people who worked at the hospital didn't know their way around the place. They'd know the places that they needed to go, but not the whole hospital. She had walked with Willie and Vic to Willie's truck to get the maps. Willie had not been able to find any parking near to the emergency entrance, of course, because there wasn't any, but he hadn't picked the same parking structure as Erin. It was on the opposite side of the hospital. Erin didn't try to cut through the hospital, it was much easier to go around the outside, even if it was longer physically.

As she walked around the building, she could hear another set of footsteps. At first, it didn't really enter her consciousness, but as she got farther away from the doors, she became more aware. Someone was headed the same direction as she was. That wasn't surprising. The hospital was teeming with people, and even that late, there were plenty of people who were coming and going to the parking structures.

Choosing to go around the hospital instead of through it might not have been the safest choice. The parking lots were not well-lit and, since most people did travel through the hospital rather than around it, there were not a lot of people outside. The farther she went around the hospital, the darker and quieter it became. Erin swallowed and clutched the maps to her and tried to breathe normally. There was no point in getting worked up over nothing.

She thought of Beaver's gun. Vic had encouraged Erin to get a gun and go target shooting with her for some time, but Erin just didn't feel comfortable about guns. Walking by herself in the dark and lonely parking lots around the hospital, she suddenly wished that she had made a different decision. She wished she had at least something in her purse that could be used as a weapon. Maybe not a gun, but at least pepper spray or a taser. She should have had Terry or Beaver escort her to her car. Everybody had gone their different directions without paying any attention to the possible dangers. The hospital was busy; who was going to get mugged there?

Erin sped up her pace, looking behind her to reassure herself that it was just another visitor like her, going back to his car. It was too dark to get a good look at the person behind her in just a quick glance, and she wasn't going to turn around for long enough to get a good look.

## APPLE-ACHIAN TREASURE

Her heart was pounding and she was breathing heavily, unable to get enough oxygen. She wasn't even close to her car. Where was a security guard? Wasn't there anyone patrolling the area outside the hospital?

Erin spotted a side door and broke into a run to reach it. She wrenched the door open and jumped back into the safety of the hospital. She stopped there for a minute, trying to catch her breath and calm the wild pounding of her heart.

She was fine, safely inside the hospital again. Perfectly safe.

She started walking again, more relaxed, chuckling at herself for being so paranoid just because someone was walking behind her in the dark. Inside where it was bright and she could hear the constant hum of voices and see people hurrying from one hall to another, she felt much better.

Erin went back to navigating the signage to find her way back to the parking structure she had parked in. She asked for directions a couple of times along the way, trying to avoid getting lost.

As she was leaving the hospital once more in the final stretch to the parking structure, Erin spotted a security guard.

"Oh, hey! Would you be able to walk me to my car? I was a little nervous earlier that someone was following me." She gave a little self-deprecating laugh. "I'm just over here in D-East." She pointed.

The guard looked at her for a moment, not answering.

"I guess maybe you have certain rounds you're supposed to do. I was just hoping maybe you could go this way…"

"Of course." He smiled and nodded. He had a big flashlight on his belt that he pulled out and clicked on. Comforted by his presence, Erin calmed down and walked with him into the parking garage. He stayed with her while she found her level and parking space.

"Thanks so much," Erin told him gratefully. "I really appreciate it."

He nodded and gave her a salute with his flashlight, then turned and walked back out.

Erin fumbled for her keys, having difficulty finding them in her purse in the dimness of the garage. She should have had the security guard shine his flashlight on them before he left. She put her maps on top of the car so that she would have both hands free to look for the keys, and eventually managed to tease them out and juggle them to find the car key.

"There you are," she said softly, and fit it into the lock.

Suddenly she was struck with a blinding pain in the back of her skull and fell forward against the car. She tried to hold herself up, but her knees buckled and she hit the pavement. Erin tried to sort out the sensations.

A shape beside her.

The purse being yanked off of her shoulder.

And then running footsteps.

# Chapter Thirteen

ERIN CLOSED HER EYES, the world spinning around her. What had just happened?

It was dark and cold on the ground. She had a splitting headache. No matter how hard she tried, she couldn't seem to get to her feet, even holding on to the car. The lighting of the garage, which had previously seemed dim, had grown blindingly bright. She reached up the car door, feeling for her keys. Had whoever had taken her purse taken the keys too? They hadn't taken the car, at least.

Erin's fingers touched the keys. She pulled the key out of the lock and felt the fob for the panic alarm. She had set it off by accident more than once, but now that she needed it, the key fob felt foreign in her fingers. Erin concentrated, running her nail over it, feeling for the cracks of the buttons. One of them had braille over it, but that wasn't the alarm key. She couldn't remember the layout of the buttons. Erin mashed her thumb down, catching all of the buttons at the same time, and held them all down until the car alarm started to shriek.

She sat leaning against the car. It was a long time before anyone came around to check on the alarm. People were too accustomed to hearing car alarms ringing for no reason. They just tuned them out. Erin knew she usually did. When she noticed a car alarm, it wasn't usually with any sort of concern, but with irritation that someone hadn't turned it off.

Then there was a man standing over her, calling to her. "Ma'am? Ma'am, are you okay?"

Erin groaned. "Does it look like it?"

"I'm calling for help. Just hang in there."

What else was she supposed to do?

"Sure," Erin muttered.

He talked on his radio to his dispatcher, relaying their location.

"Did you fall down?" he asked her. "What happened? Does it hurt anywhere?"

"My head. Someone stole my purse. I think they hit me on the head."

He muttered a curse and crouched down beside her, pulling her head back gently from the car to have a look at it. "Oh, yeah. He hit you."

There was a stabbing pain and the spinning sensation increased. Erin moaned. "Don't do that."

He released her head slowly, letting it rest back against the car again, where she was sitting propped up.

"Did you see him? The person who did this?"

"No. I don't have eyes in the back of my head."

"Of course not," he agreed. He checked in on his radio again, asking for an ETA on the paramedics. "They're coming," he reported back. "Hang in there."

She thought he might be the same guard who had walked her into the parking garage.

Time was fuzzy. She didn't know how long she waited there, the man talking to her occasionally, before she finally heard the ambulance siren. Had they actually dispatched it from somewhere else? They were at the hospital, but no one could just come out to help her?

The man waved down the ambulance and reported Erin's condition to her as he walked them over. Erin listened to him describe the injury to her head and her state of responsiveness. The paramedics came over and had a look for themselves.

"Yep, pretty good blow to the head," one of them confirmed. "How are you doing, ma'am? Are you in a lot of pain?"

"Yes."

He worked over her, evaluating her as they talked, checking her pulse and her eyes.

"Can you stand up if we help you?"

Erin avoided shaking her head. "No."

"Okay, we'll get the gurney over here and get you onto it. How long ago did this happen, do you know? Do you know what day it is?"

Erin cleared her throat. Too many questions too fast. "Just give me something for the pain."

"We'll let the hospital do that once we get you stabilized. Can you tell me what day it is?"

"I don't know. Wednesday. Not the weekend."

"Can you tell me your first and last name?"

"Erin. Uh. Erin Price. Price."

"What were you doing here today, Erin?"

"My friend… her brother got shot. I brought her over and was sitting with her."

"Ouch. Don't like to hear that. Was he okay?"

"Yeah. Okay. They said he'd be fine."

"Good. Let's get that gurney over here and get you onto it. How's your neck? Feeling okay?"

"Yeah."

They prepared to move Erin. She looked at her car shining softly in the lighting of the parking garage and wondered what she was doing there.

"I need to get home," she told the paramedic preparing to lift her.

He looked down at her and raised one eyebrow. "You'll get home, but we need to take care of you first. I don't think you're going to be going anywhere tonight."

"But I have to get to the bakery in the morning. I need to go home and get some sleep."

"You'll be able to sleep here. Let's see how you feel when you wake up in the morning, huh?"

That seemed to make some kind of sense. Erin nodded, which made her feel drunk.

"Okay."

"Okay, honey. Now let's get you moving."

The two of them managed to lift her up onto the gurney, and they rolled her inside the ambulance. Erin looked around. She couldn't remember ever being in an ambulance before.

She must have been in one after the accident that took her parents' lives. It had been just the three of them, and they were all taken to the hospital. But Erin couldn't remember the details. Maybe she had been unconscious. Or maybe it had just been too traumatic or was too long ago.

"Do you think I'll remember this time?" she asked the paramedic who climbed in beside her.

"Remember what, sweetheart?"

"That I rode in an ambulance."

"Hmm. Maybe, maybe not. I think you're pretty shaken up."

"Yeah."

"Just rest for a bit. Even though we're already at the hospital, this is still going to take a while."

"Okay."

But Erin didn't like the way the world spun even faster when she closed her eyes, so she kept them open, watching everything sway around her as the ambulance made its way back around the hospital to the emergency entrance. Around, and around, and around. She couldn't seem to get away from the hospital.

"The Hotel California," Erin murmured.

The paramedic grinned at her but didn't say anything.

They went back around to the ambulance loading bay, and the paramedics took her into the hospital. There, Erin

# APPLE-ACHIAN TREASURE

was expected to answer their questions all over again, but they didn't seem inclined to answer any of hers.

"When can I go home?" Erin demanded. "I need to get home."

"You need to just rest and let us help you," a large black nurse told her sternly.

Erin was cowed by her and tried to stay quiet. But she was confused by everything going on around her. "Is Jeremy okay?"

"Jeremy? Who is Jeremy?"

"He was shot. He was here earlier."

"Oh, the GSW that came in on the last shift? I don't know. Sounded like he was doing okay. We don't really hear back after they go to surgery."

"The doctor said he was okay."

"Then you don't need to worry about him, do you? Can you tell me your birth date?"

Erin had a hard time dredging it out of her memory.

"How about your social security number?"

Erin gave her head a tiny shake. "No, I could never remember it. My purse…"

The nurse looked around. "I don't think you were brought in with one."

"Someone stole it."

"Oh, dear. Is that how you got hit on the head? You poor thing."

There was a red light blinking on a camera in the corner of the room, and Erin wondered if they were going to show her a video. She did her best to stay focused on what they were saying around her, but she was getting very tired and the nausea and vertigo were not helping.

"Can I go to sleep?"

"You can," one nurse said, patting her hand, "but someone will probably wake you up again. Just be warned."

"Okay."

Erin closed her eyes and drifted off.

There were doctors and nurses coming and going in a sort of a blur, but when she woke up fully the next time, it was to Terry shaking her arm. Erin startled and looked at him.

"What time is it? I'm going to be late opening the bakery!"

"It's okay," he assured her. "Don't worry about the bakery. What happened? I called you and you didn't answer. I was afraid you fell asleep at the wheel and went off the road."

"I didn't fall asleep," Erin said. "I didn't go to sleep until I was here, and the nurse said it was okay. I asked."

"What happened?"

"Someone stole my purse. They hit me on the head. I was in the garage."

"You were mugged?"

"Yes."

"You really are a magnet for trouble." Terry stroked her chin gently with the backs of his fingers. "My poor girl."

Erin closed her eyes. "That feels good."

"I shouldn't have let you walk to your car alone. I didn't even think about the danger... It's so dark and lonely at night..."

"I didn't walk alone. I had a security guard."

"You did? You had someone escort you to your car?"

"Yeah. Someone was following me. I was worried... I didn't want anything to happen to me too, so I went back in and I asked."

Terry nodded. "That was a smart thing to do. So, what happened? It wasn't the guard who hurt you, was it?"

Erin thought about it. "No. He didn't see anyone there... neither of us saw anybody... so he left. I just had to get into my car."

"But there *was* someone there."

"I never saw him coming. He just hit me."

"You didn't see who did it? Get a look at his face?" Terry asked.

"No. He hit me from behind. I didn't even know there was anyone there until he hit me. I felt like I got hit by a truck."

"Did you see him after? Running away?"

"No…" Erin thought about it. "I heard him. I might have seen a shape. Just a dark shape. But I didn't ever see his face. He made sure of that."

"His footsteps when he ran away, did they sound like he was tall or short?"

"I don't know. Tall. Maybe."

"And the person who scared you earlier, who you thought might be following you? Did you get a good look at him?"

"No, not close enough to even tell if it was a man or a woman. Actually, I'm sure it was a man, but I'm not sure how."

"You might have been able to tell from his gait or his smell. His shape or the clothes he wore. It's easy to be wrong, but if you had an impression, at least that's something."

"I guess."

Erin thought about smell. She was usually good about smells. Was that what had suggested to her it was a man? A musky cologne or male body odor? Pheromones?

Had it been the same person who had followed her both times, or had it just been a coincidence? Had she made herself a target by looking too vulnerable?

"Erin?"

She realized that she had been drifting off. She tried to sit up. Terry readjusted her pillow, but it was flat and didn't give her any lift. Erin wasn't in a permanent bed yet and she didn't know if they could raise the head of the bed. Or if she really wanted them to. She might just want to go back to sleep.

"Will they look for my purse?" she asked Terry. "I mean, after he's got what he wants, he'll just dump it, won't he? I have other things in there I want back."

"I'll make sure they look. Actually, I might be able to track your phone. I can see where he is if he has it or where it is if he dumped it."

"That would be good," Erin agreed. She didn't like the idea of someone else having her stuff. Or of their just dumping it like it was garbage. Having been a foster kid without any possessions of her own to speak of she grew attached to things. It was hard to let go.

"I need a notepad."

Terry frowned. "A notepad? What for?"

"I just… I might want to write things down. And I need a notepad to write them in."

Terry patted his clothes. He pulled a small spiral notepad out of his shirt pocket and tore a few sheets out. He put them on the small table beside her, putting a pencil on top to keep them from flying away when someone walked by and stirred the air. "It isn't much, but it will do in a pinch," he said. "I'll get you something better if I can't find your purse."

Erin let out a sigh. Anyone else probably would have teased her or would have told her it wasn't important and that she didn't need to write anything down. But Terry knew how important it was for her to be able to get her thoughts down on paper to sort them out. He was a good man. "Thank you," she told him, her eyes warm with tears.

"You're welcome. Do you want me to stay here with you, or do you want me to see if I can find your phone and purse?"

"I think I'm just going to close my eyes for a while longer. Would you see if you can find them?"

"Sure." Terry bent down and gave her a kiss on the forehead. "You have a good rest. I'll be back in a little while." He smiled. "Don't you go getting into any other trouble while I'm gone."

"I won't."

There was a lot of talking and commotion and people going back and forth holding discussions in loud voices, and Erin didn't know how she was going to be able to shut them out and get any rest but, in a few minutes, she was asleep again, or at least in a half-asleep state, her mind jumping from one thing to another, not constrained by the real world.

A few doctors or nurses spoke to her. Erin wasn't sure if she made any sense when she answered them, because she couldn't remember the conversations afterward. There was another policeman who wasn't Terry. Too many people coming and going.

She didn't know what time it was when she was finally moved out of the emergency room into a ward where it was quieter and she could sleep for real. Or at least, she was moved into the hallway of a ward, which apparently didn't have any free beds for her. But she was just glad to be out of the high-traffic emergency room.

It was much quieter and more peaceful. She closed her eyes and was able to get past the half-sleep state into a more restful sleep.

# Chapter Fourteen

WHEN ERIN WOKE UP, Terry was asleep in a chair nearby, which he had apparently pulled from some other room in order to be close to her. K9 was lying on the floor at his feet, also asleep. Erin moved around restlessly, trying to find the comfortable position she had just been in, but her whole body ached and was insisting that she needed to move around and stretch her muscles. Any position she tried to settle into, she felt like she was lying on lumps and bruises.

There was something stuffed beside her on the bed, and when Erin craned her neck to see what it was, she saw her purse. She pulled it up onto her stomach and went through it to see what was there and what was missing. Everything seemed to be accounted for other than her cash. Even her phone and credit cards were still there.

Her movements apparently woke K9, and he nudged Terry awake. Terry looked over at Erin and gave her a sleepy, concerned smile. The dimple in his cheek was just visible. "There's my girl. Did you get some sleep?"

"A little."

"Can you tell if anything is missing?" He nodded to her purse.

"Just my cash. Everything else still seems to be there."

He shook his head. "Lazy muggers. If he's going to go to all of the work of knocking someone down, he could at least try to make use of the credit cards and the phone."

## APPLE-ACHIAN TREASURE

Erin chuckled. "I'm glad he didn't. There wasn't even that much cash in it. If he needs it that badly, then he's welcome to it. I wish he'd asked instead of hitting me over the head."

"I put your keys in there too, after checking out your car to make sure everything was undisturbed. It doesn't look like he even opened the door."

"No," Erin agreed. "I was just unlocking it when he hit me, and he ran away without trying it. I guess I was lucky."

"He might still have gone back once the paramedics took you away. Was there anything valuable in the car?"

"No. I don't keep anything in there. I just..." Erin thought about her movements the night before, replaying it in her mind, feeling like she was missing something important. "No, I just..."

Terry studied her, waiting for her to work it out.

"I just put Willie's maps on top of the car so that I could use both hands to get out my keys. Were they still there?"

He shook his head. "No, I didn't see any maps. What were they for?"

"For the you-know-what." Erin looked around to make sure no one was listening in. "Willie said to be careful about talking about it here. You know, the poem, and where it leads."

"Oh." Terry's face cleared and he nodded. "I got it."

Erin looked down at her purse again, frowning. She looked through the loose papers that she tried to keep organized with envelopes and paperclips but couldn't find it.

"That's... it's missing. He *didn't* just take the money."

"What else is missing?"

"The poem."

Erin was waiting for word from the doctor that she could be discharged when Vic walked in, pushing Jeremy in a wheelchair. He was dressed in a hospital johnny, but looked remarkably well, as if it were just a Halloween costume.

"Vic! Jeremy! How are you?"

"I am just as good as you, if not better," Jeremy said with a grin.

"I just got bumped on the head. You got two bullets in you."

"Yeah, but the doctor fixed me all up. You didn't get any work done. I'm good as new."

"Are you going home?"

He hesitated. "Well, not quite yet."

"Then I'm in better shape than you are. I'm just waiting to be released."

"That's because you've got someone to take care of you when you get home. You've got Vic and Terry around, so you're not on your own."

"What about Beaver? Can't she look after you?"

"No, she's got to get back to work. She won't be able to stay close by like Terry and Vic."

"They've got to work too," Erin said. "Though if I called them, they could come. But I'm not going to need to do that, because I'll be back at work, not at home."

"You're not ready to go back to work," Vic said sternly.

"I have to! We have to keep the bakery running."

"We'll keep the bakery running. You need to stay home until you're healed. You're not allowed to come back in while you're still concussed."

"Why not? It's not affecting me. Other people would be around."

"For the same reason you're not allowed to drive," Vic said. "You need to do what the doctors say."

"They didn't say I couldn't drive or work."

"Well, I'm saying it."

Erin rolled her eyes. "How are you feeling?" she asked Jeremy, cocking her head to look at him. "You sure are looking a lot better than I would have expected."

"I'm sore all over," Jeremy admitted. "Apparently, getting shot is sort of the equivalent of being trampled by a horse. I'm not just sore where the bullets went in, it's like I have the flu or got beaten up."

"Me too. I only got hit once, on the head, but I feel like he must have punched and kicked me once I went down, because everything is tender. Every time I move, I find a new bruise or sore muscle."

Jeremy nodded. "We make a good pair. Maybe we should both just go back to your place and we can take care of each other and commiserate over our injuries."

Erin looked over at Vic, who shook her head.

"I don't think that's a good idea. Jeremy's not ready to go home yet, even if he thinks he is. If one of you fell down and needed help getting up, you'd both just end up on the floor. Neither of you is supposed to be doing any heavy lifting."

"I'm not going to fall down," Erin said.

"Neither am I," Jeremy agreed.

"You guys are incorrigible. Quit it. Besides," Vic raised an eyebrow at Erin, "I don't think your man would be too happy about Jeremy staying at your house again."

Erin shrugged stiffly. "He might not be, but I don't make all of my decisions based on what he does or doesn't want, either. I'll do what I think is best."

Vic raised her eyebrows. "Well, I don't think I've heard you talk that way about Terry before. Are you sure it's not the concussion talking?"

"No… it's me. I know he doesn't like everything I do. But I'm my own person. I'll do what I need to do."

Vic nodded. "I've always said so. Good for you. If he's expecting you to be some shrinking violet who does everything she is told and just stays in the kitchen all day, he should think again. You might act like a pushover sometimes, but underneath, you're pretty tough."

Jeremy looked at Vic, frowning. He looked back at Erin.

"I don't know if women like being classified as tough any more than as a shrinking violet, do they?"

Vic shrugged. "It depends on the woman. I'd rather be tough than a cupcake. I think Beaver would say the same thing. Erin might like cupcakes, but I don't think she wants to be one."

Erin laughed at that. "No, I don't," she agreed. "I am my own person. I don't know why Terry is acting like he owns me or can control what I do. I'm not a child."

"He just wants to protect you," Jeremy said. "He's a cop. It's in his DNA. He wants to protect people, and especially the ones closest to him. He's not telling you that you can't be the person you want to be, he just wants to keep you from getting hurt and is trying to encourage you down the pathway he thinks is safest."

"He can't keep bad things from happening," Erin pointed out. "No matter what he does, he can't predict the future and he can't keep things from happening to me, or Vic, or even himself. You can go down all the safe garden paths you like, but that doesn't keep you from being run over by a bus."

"Or hit by a mugger," Jeremy agreed.

"Or shot by a poacher," Vic added.

"It's just not feasible to avoid every danger."

"Of course not," Jeremy agreed. "But that doesn't mean Terry won't try. And as far as me staying at the house with you… well, it's perfectly understandable that he doesn't want another guy horning in on his territory. Even if you're not his *territory*. I know he doesn't own you. But he doesn't want another guy looking at you. Trying to have a relationship with you."

"Well, I told him that wasn't the case. You were just a friend staying over for a few days. I told him there wasn't anything between us, but he still gets all… manly about it."

## APPLE-ACHIAN TREASURE

Vic laughed. "Well, you wouldn't want him to stop being manly, would you? I don't think you would have picked a cop in uniform if you didn't like that about him."

Erin's face warmed. She rolled her eyes and looked around the room, looking for some way to change the subject.

"Personal preferences aside... I do want to talk about the schedule at Auntie Clem's. We can't let it just stay closed until I'm feeling better. I don't know how many days it will be before I can put in a full day. I might only be able to come in for a few hours at a time at first, until I'm sure that I've got my mojo back."

"Don't worry about it," Vic said. "We'll take care of everything. Bella was in early this morning and Charley is taking over at noon. Then I'll do late shift and make sure everything is prepped again for the morning. It's not as easy to run the shop with just one person on shift at a time, but it's possible, especially if we're not putting in full-length shifts. You can put up with it being harder if you know you don't have to be there as long. We might work it so that we overlap by an hour over the usual rushes; we'll put our heads together and see what we can come up with. In the meantime, you're not allowed to worry about anything. You just rest and be reassured that we're holding things together until you're healthy again. Really healthy, not forcing yourself to come back because you're afraid everything is going to fall apart."

"Are you sure?" Erin was already worrying about how hard it would be for each of them to run the bakery by themselves. She had done everything by herself for the first little while, before taking Vic on as an employee, and it had been exhausting. There had to be a way to set up the shifts so that two people could cover each shift...

"Leave it to me," Vic insisted, staring at Erin as if she could see right into her mind to what she was thinking. "You don't need to think about it at all. Bella is happy to take the early shift. She doesn't have any classes that interfere and she's a farm girl, so she's used to being up early. Obviously, Charley can't take the early shift, but she's fine once she's out of bed. She doesn't even have to make anything for the middle shift, she can just man the counter. But she likes to cook, so I think she'll still put in a tray of cookies when she has a lull. Then I'm there at the end of the day to make sure that everything is cleaned up to your usual exacting standards and that all of the batters are ready for when Bella gets there in the morning. We all get our preferred time of day, I still have time to check in on Jeremy or you, and nobody is trying to shoulder the full burden."

"I suppose." Erin had to admit, it sounded like they had everything worked out. She wanted to fix it, but if there was nothing to fix, she should just let them do it their way and not try to come up with a better idea.

"Why don't you work on the mystery while you're recovering?" Jeremy suggested. "You can look at the poem and see where the clues lead you. Maybe you'll be able to find something out that you weren't able to see before, when you were so busy and distracted by other things."

Vic bit her lip and gave Jeremy a warning look.

"What?" Jeremy shook his head, eyebrows down. "What did I say?"

"Terry told me. When Erin got mugged, they stole the poem and Willie's maps."

Jeremy looked surprised. He opened his mouth to speak, then did a sort of double-take and looked at Vic again, opening and closing his mouth like a fish on the other side of the aquarium glass.

"Yeah," Vic confirmed. "Someone else is trying to find the treasure. Someone who is willing to hurt people to find it."

# Chapter Fifteen

As far as Terry was concerned, and probably the rest of the men who were her friends too, Erin should just drop the treasure hunt nonsense and do something that was safer. But as Erin had said, she wasn't about to live her life the way that Terry or anyone else said that she should. She had always found her own path in the world and was her own person, and that wasn't going to stop. She wasn't going to be cowed just because someone had hit her over the head and taken the poem and the maps.

Willie said that he hadn't given her the original maps, just good quality copies, which he could run off again and, while Erin hadn't made any copies of the poem, she had read it enough times that she had it memorized. As soon as she got home and was alone, she wrote it out again, just the same as it had been on the original. Maybe not exactly the same, because she couldn't replicate exactly the swoops and curls of the old-fashioned script that it had been written in, but she did the best she could to keep the spacing the same and to exactly replicate each word and mark that had been on the original paper in case there was any significance in the way they lined up.

She wasn't going to give up on finding the treasure. Maybe someone else was looking for it, but that didn't mean she was just going to go away. She had a head start on whoever was just picking up the hunt. Maybe it was only a few days of research, but she knew more than they did, and that meant she could get to the treasure faster.

She studied the words of the poem. She couldn't do much about the maps until Willie got her new copies. She had looked at them only briefly, and she had only a rough idea of the topography and roads from what Betty and Edna had drawn for her, but it was enough for a start.

She went back to Clementine's files and thumbed through the labels on the folders. Nothing on lost treasure. Nothing on old legends or untold riches. But she might have something in one of her files that would point Erin in the right direction.

She started at the front of the drawer and looked carefully at each folder, rating them as to which was most likely to hold clues to the treasure hunt poem, and then she went through each of the likely folders from front to back, examining every single page and clipping carefully. She had all the time she needed.

She had all day for as many days as she decided to tell her employees that she needed to be home, and they would keep the bakery running in her absence. She wouldn't draw it out any longer than she needed to, of course, but she could take all the time she needed, and why not do something productive with it?

"Here, look at this." Erin knew that Vic was tired and probably just wanted to get into a hot shower and some comfy clothes for the evening. She'd be up at the hospital again in the morning to check on Jeremy and see if he needed anything. Even if she wasn't working her usual long hours, she was still keeping herself busy for most of the day. "It will only take a minute."

Vic sat down to look at the file Erin had pulled out.

"This is a file on Orson Cadaver."

Vic's eyes widened and she opened her mouth to make a crack about the name.

# APPLE-ACHIAN TREASURE

"I know," Erin said, "spooky name, right? Anyway, this is a great, great-something uncle of mine. He was raised dirt poor, never had a single possession, and then suddenly he starts spending a fortune in gold coins."

Vic took the folder from her and read through the first paper or two. "It was modern currency, not like he dug up a pirate treasure."

"I know. It was modern, and he said he earned it legitimately. But get this—he would never say how he earned it. Just that it had been honest work. But with the amounts of money that he had suddenly come into, everybody thought he'd robbed a wagon train or hit it big in the mines. Or that he found a pirate treasure and cashed it in for modern gold. He would have had to pass it through someone else to get it laundered. No one knew for sure how he had gotten the money in the first place."

"That is kind of suspicious," Vic admitted. "Where did he live? Right here in Bald Eagle Falls?"

"No, down in the valley. He'd been trying to farm, but there wasn't enough flatland. The soil was the wrong pH or something and wouldn't grow corn or the other crops he tried. He did something else every year, and just got further and further behind. Then suddenly, he is successful, but he won't tell anyone what it was he planted, and no one knew what it was he took to market. He drove wagonloads of product into the market for sale, but it was covered up and nobody knew who he sold to or what commodity it was he was selling."

"Maybe he was a witch," Vic suggested. "It all sounds pretty dark and mysterious."

"A witch?" Erin repeated.

"You know, selling potions or elixirs or turning coal into gold. Something sinister and unexplainable."

Erin gave Vic a look. They both knew that Adele, an actual witch, didn't do anything of the sort. "I think he might actually have found the gold for the corn crops. Or the soldiers' payroll that disappeared. The timing is right. Of course, he never says so, because neither one was intended for him. But if he had been lying in wait along one of those routes that Edna pointed out…"

"It would take more than one man to take down all of the guards transporting a big payment like that. They wouldn't have sent it on its way without lots of protection."

"Maybe he had help. Maybe he hired someone else to help him. If he did, we don't know what happened to them. Either he paid them off well so that they wouldn't talk about it, or he got rid of them some other way."

Vic gave a shudder. "You really think this is the guy? He's the one who hid the treasure?"

"It makes sense. I haven't come across anyone else in the family who suddenly had more money than they should have. This guy was as poor as dirt before this, then suddenly starts paying for everything with gold coins. They had to come from somewhere, but he would never say where. And he didn't have any heirs. After he died, people went looking for his money. They found a few gold coins, but no fortune. Like they just found his spending money, but the real money was somewhere else."

"Like the bank, maybe? Why didn't these guys ever use banks?"

"Maybe they weren't secure then like they are now. Or they weren't being run by someone trustworthy. Weren't insured. Things weren't regulated like they are now, were they?"

"No, you're right there," Vic admitted. "But if they all looked for it at the time, then what makes you think that we're going to find anything now? They would have looked pretty carefully."

"But they didn't have the poem."

"If the poem is related to Orson, then why wasn't it in that file instead of the one you found it in?"

# APPLE-ACHIAN TREASURE

"I don't know. Maybe Clementine didn't know they were related. Or maybe she didn't want someone else to know."

"Or maybe they're not related."

Erin shrugged. "Maybe not, but looking is fun, isn't it?"

Vic laughed. "It is, kind of. So, what's your next step?"

"As soon as I get the maps from Willie, we go down to see if we can find Orson's old house. I think there's enough detail in this file to identify where it is once we have the map. And then… maybe we find more clues."

# Chapter Sixteen

It was a few days before Erin was able to get away with Vic to try to find Orson's old homestead. She had to first convince everybody that she was well enough to be working again, and then, once she was well enough to work, she had to be at Auntie Clem's doing her job until she could arrange for a day off for both her and Vic. Since everybody had been putting in extra hours, it didn't seem right for Erin to take the first opportunity to get a shift off again. But when Saturday afternoon rolled around, Bella was happy to take a quiet shift and let Erin and Vic go off treasure hunting. Though they didn't tell her that was what they were going to do. They might have led her to believe they were going into the city to visit Jeremy or to take him out on a day trip. Jeremy *was* getting pretty eager to get out of the hospital, feeling like he could be back to his normal activities again in spite of the gunshot wounds.

"Do you think we'll be able to find it?" Erin asked, as Vic followed her instructions through the overgrown backroads to try to find the old homestead.

"If it's there, we'll find it," Vic said. "The cabin, that is. I'm not guaranteeing anything else."

"We don't even know if there *is* anything else," Erin said agreeably. "Who knows?"

"Right. If it's still standing, we'll find the cabin."

# APPLE-ACHIAN TREASURE

Erin studied the survey map closely. It wasn't easy to compare the roads and trees they were passing with the flat survey map and to match everything up properly. "I think there should be another road to the right, about three hundred yards ahead."

"Okay…" Vic was already going pretty slowly, but she hit the brake and they both watched for a break in the trees where there might be an access road. Some of the roads they had taken to get there had been pretty questionable. They might have been roads at one time, but Erin wasn't sure that they could be called roads anymore.

"There."

Vic turned the car slowly in. "Maybe we should have waited and gotten one of the boys to come with their trucks. I'm a little worried about your car's suspension handling this off-roading."

"We're not off-roading," Erin corrected. "These are roads. They're just very… not very well-maintained anymore. They've been replaced by paved highways, so people don't really use them anymore."

"Not very well-maintained." Vic snorted. "You have a talent for understatement."

Erin grinned. She looked back down at the map, trying to pick out landmarks, topography, and distances. "We'll go in a curve around a hill, and when we get to the opposite side, there should be a fork in the road, and we're to take the left one."

"Left fork," Vic confirmed. They again watched intently out the windshield as the barely-visible track wound around the hill. "Here? Is that a fork?"

"I don't know. It could be." Erin tried to compare it with the map. "Let's give it a try."

"Are you going to get me lost?"

"We can't get lost; we have a map."

"That doesn't mean we know where we are."

"We know where we are. We're... somewhere on this map. Somewhere on one of these maps." Erin shuffled through them. "We're not going to get lost."

"Don't lose track of which one we're supposed to be on," Vic said nervously.

"I'm not going to mix them up. We're on this top one. Or was it this one?" Erin looked slyly sideways at Vic, who shook her head at Erin baiting her.

"Okay, where after this?"

"Looks like about two miles. We just keep following this road. And then eventually, we'll be up to Orson's house."

"I sure hope it's still there," Vic said. "I don't see much other development out here. Doesn't look like anybody is even farming this land anymore. So hopefully…"

Erin looked at the land with new eyes. There were areas that were clear of trees and the land was fairly flat. But she wasn't sure she would have tried to farm it. It would have taken a lot of work to plow the land, breaking the soil and moving the rocks out of the fields, trying to keep the trees from creeping back in on them.

"This really is wild," she said.

"Yeah, it is," Vic said. "A lot more remote than my farm."

Erin remembered Vic's family farm. It had been more like the farms she was accustomed to; much flatter, with a country farmhouse and a big red barn.

They were both watching the odometer to see how far they had gone. Erin looked out the window and started scanning for any buildings or fences or signs of the old farm. The country looked untouched other than the faint track through the trees that Vic was trying to follow without jostling their brains out. Erin was starting to regret having tried to find the house so soon. She was still having headaches following her mugging and the bumps and ruts in the so-called road were not helping.

"What's that?" Vic pointed.

# APPLE-ACHIAN TREASURE

Erin could barely see the outline through the trees. "Is it a house? I think it's a house! I think that's it!"

Vic got as close as she could. The trees were doing their best to take back the clearing that had once been made, and they couldn't drive right up to the house. It was very small, and Erin was worried it was just an outhouse or shed until they got closer. It was larger than it looked from the road, but still very small when compared to Clementine's house or most of the homes that Erin had grown up in.

"It guess this is it," she said, looking around for any other buildings. If there had been barns and other outbuildings, they had been reclaimed by nature; Erin couldn't see any sign of them. The house must have been sturdily built to have resisted the advances of time.

Vic parked the car. They both got out, looking around. There was no sign of other human life around them. The birds were singing and the sun was shining. The leaves were rustling in a slight wind. But it seemed like it had been a hundred years since another human being had set foot on the property.

"Just look at it," Vic breathed.

They walked toward the house. Old and gray from the weather, but the corners still mostly square. The windows were broken and a couple had tattered curtains behind them. As they got closer, Vic called out.

"Hallo the house! Anyone home?"

Erin looked at her.

"There's no one here. That's obvious."

"Well... it's still rude to just walk in."

"Even if there's nobody there?"

Vic shrugged. "What can I tell you? Even if you don't think there's anyone home, you should always call just to be sure. I was always taught that."

"Okay!" Erin laughed and continued to walk toward the house.

There was still no answer, but neither expected there to be. Erin expected Vic to knock on the door when they got to it, further demonstrating her training in southern manners, but Vic did not. She put her hand on the doorknob and waited for a moment.

"Do you want to open it?" she asked. "He's your uncle."

"Go ahead."

"On the count of three?"

Erin again laughed and waited for Vic to count it off and open the door. It wasn't locked and swung open under her hand. They walked in and looked around the interior of the house.

It was empty. Any furniture that had once been in the house was long gone, other than a kitchen table made of a slab of wood, and a broken-down rocking chair across the room by the fireplace. It was mostly a one-room home, with partial partitions built up between the kitchen and the seating area, and a little niche Erin thought must have been for a bed. Very small and cozy. Even smaller than the summerhouse on Erin's property that Adele lived in.

"See any clues?" Vic asked.

Erin searched the room. There was no desk with hidden compartments. There were no cryptic notes scribbled on the walls. Anything that had been left in the house was long gone.

She walked around the little room, looking at the plank wall, where there could obviously be no hidden rooms. In places there were wide cracks between the planks where the sun came in from the outside.

"There's something there," Erin pointed to the floor at a cut-out square.

"A trapdoor," Vic observed. "There must be a root cellar."

They went over to it together. Vic put her finger into a little notch cut-out and gave a tug. The trapdoor no longer fit well in the space. It took a bit of pulling and tugging

## APPLE-ACHIAN TREASURE

before Vic was able to lever it up. Erin looked at the narrow stairs that led down into the darkness. It was more like a ladder than a staircase. Erin wasn't sure how anyone would walk down it.

"You want to go down?" Vic asked.

"It's worse than the basement at Bella's house."

"Definitely."

Neither one of them made any move to go down the steps to see what was down there.

"If there are any clues, they're going to be down there," Vic said. "You can see there isn't anything left up here."

Erin looked around. She looked up at the roof of the house. No attic, just the inside of the roof that kept out the rain. Or mostly, anyway. They could go outside and look for a barn and other outbuildings. There might be more clues as to what Orson Cadaver had been doing in the outbuildings. Erin hadn't been able to see any from the car, but that didn't mean they didn't exist. One just had to look harder.

"You want me to go first?" Vic asked.

"Yes."

"If I go down there, you have to too."

"I don't know about that."

"Come on, Erin. You can do that. It's not a cave, it's just a basement. And there won't be any hidden corners. You'll be able to see everything when you get down the stairs."

Erin crouched down at the edge of the hole. "Maybe I could just poke my head down and not go down at all."

"I'll go first, but only if you promise you'll come too."

Erin let out a puff of breath. "Fine. I'll go down. Unless you fall and break your leg. Then I'm going back to the car to get help."

"I'm not going to break my leg."

"You might. Those stairs don't look very safe."

Vic stopped arguing and walked around the trapdoor, trying to figure out the best way to get down the dangerous-looking stairs. She finally decided to approach it like a ladder. She went down it backward, feet first, holding on to the sides of the stairway to stabilize herself.

When she got to the bottom, she put her foot out to feel for another step, then looked down and saw that she had made it. She pushed away from the stairs and looked around.

"Come on down."

"Is there anything to see?"

"Erin you promised you'd come. So, come."

Erin hesitated. But she had promised, so she slowly climbed down the stairs the same way as Vic had. They held their phones up with flashlight apps on to explore the tiny cellar.

"Not much here," Erin muttered.

"Nope."

It was a dirt floor. There were a couple of shelves that might have once held preserves. There was a wooden plank box with a lid torn off. Erin bent over it, shining her light into the box.

There were a few twisted shapes. Old parsnips and potatoes or other roots that Erin wasn't sure about that had dried out and petrified long ago. She poked around at them with one finger, worried about stirring up spiders or something worse. Nothing jumped out at her. There was no journal or note or other clue hidden under the old vegetables.

Erin stood back up. "Well… let's explore a little more upstairs and outside. Maybe there are some other buildings that might give us a clue."

## Chapter Seventeen

The upstairs was no more enlightening than it had been the first time they looked at it. Erin looked again for any hidden panels, notes folded up and stuffed into the cracks of boards, or anything else that might give them a clue as to the hiding place of old Orson's fabled gold. There was nothing in the house.

Outside, Erin looked out at the forest. If Orson had indeed cleared a field, it was barely detectable a hundred and fifty years later. The trees had reclaimed the area.

There was a scattering of low plants with bright yellow leaves dappling the shadows under the trees. Tennessee autumn came much later than Erin was used to in Maine, but she had noticed some changes and variations in the foliage.

"I'm going to get the map." Erin returned to the car to get the map to see if there were any other buildings or landmarks marked on it that they should look at.

Erin returned to where Vic was standing.

"Do you see anything?" she asked.

Vic motioned to the trees to their right. "I think there's a building over there. Maybe some pieces of an old barn."

Erin squinted, but couldn't see anything through the trees that looked like a building. She looked at the map in her hand, then she and Vic walked over to have a look. Erin had been looking for a building that was still standing, like the house, so she hadn't seen the timbers that were on the ground. They walked around the perimeter of the pile of wood pieces, looking down at the ground and the area around for anything that they might have missed.

"You want to look through this?" Vic asked, motioning to the boards. "It could take a while."

"Let's just have a quick look," Erin said. "We can look more later. If it looks promising or if we can't find anything else."

They moved in. Erin thought belatedly that they should have brought work gloves and shovels and rakes. Any other implements that would let them handle the old boards and detritus without getting dirty or putting nail holes in their hands. As it was, they handled the boards delicately, trying to avoid slivers or dirt. Or spiders or other crawly creatures that might like hiding in the pile.

"Looks like there was a fire," Vic pointed out, as they got down a layer and encountered boards that had been blackened to charcoal.

Erin agreed. "I guess that's why it's not standing anymore. If he did leave any clues here, they would have been destroyed."

"Depending on what kind of clues they were. If he left another note with a poem…" Vic wiped her forehead with the back of her arm.

"There could still be a strong box or coins. They would have survived. But chances are, whoever burned it down would already have looked through the debris for anything like that."

"It might not have been burned down deliberately. Could have been a lantern or a lightning strike. And who knows how long ago. It might have just happened last year." Vic studied the wood, looking for clues. "Longer ago than that, though, I'd say. There's a lot of overgrowth. If it was just last year, there wouldn't be so much growth over top of the site. This looks like it's been here for a long time."

## APPLE-ACHIAN TREASURE

"Yeah." Erin looked at the pile. It had been there before she was born. Before her parents or grandparents were born. A long time. It gave her a strange feeling of being small and insignificant. All of that history, all of that time marching by, and nothing had changed. She hadn't changed anything. She and her ancestors were barely a blip in the long history of the place. Nature was wiping out every trace.

She abandoned her search of the wood. If there was anything hidden in the ashes and fallen timbers of the barn, it was going to take a much more involved excavation to get at them. More people, and proper equipment rather than bare hands. She took the map back out of her pocket.

"What do you think? It looks like there were a few roads through here back in the day. But everything is so overgrown, that even the main road is almost undetectable. There's no way we're going to find any of these other roads."

Vic looked at the map, studying the lines and the contours of the topography. "Actually, I don't think those are roads."

"What are they, then? Rivers?"

Vic shook her head and looked at the title and legend on the map. "This was a mining survey. I think those are mines that were dug and then abandoned."

"I'm not going down any old mines," Erin said immediately.

"No, not today," Vic agreed. "We'll need Willie to look to see what kind of condition they are in. They might need to be shored up. Or they might be completely caved in. But we're not going to go anywhere without him having a look first to make sure it's safe."

"I'm not going into any abandoned mines period. I don't care how much money might be down there. I'm just not doing it."

"Okay. That's fine. Leave it to me and Willie."

Erin shook her head. She didn't even want any of them going into an old mine. Just the thought of it made her stomach clench. She and Jeremy had already been in the hospital; she didn't want anyone else put in danger. And she knew how dangerous it could be underground. It wasn't safe for any of them.

"Let's just see if we can find any entrances," Vic suggested. "We're definitely not going in anywhere. But if we can find the entrances and maybe take some pictures for Willie, it will save time. He'll have a better idea of what kind of shape they're in and what kind of equipment we'll need, and we won't have to waste time looking later. And if I'm wrong, and they are something other than mines, then we won't be wasting time coming back for something that isn't there."

# Chapter Eighteen

TIRED AND GRUBBY AFTER their afternoon at Orson's old farm, Erin and Vic decided to go back to the hospital before heading home to Bald Eagle Falls. It wasn't long before Jeremy would be released. Erin was looking forward to knowing that he was close to home and they could go see him just a few minutes away instead of having to take a couple of extra hours to go to the city and back. It made it quite an ordeal.

"We should stop for something to eat while we're here too," Vic suggested. "Otherwise, we're going to be too tired when we get home to do anything other than put something in the microwave." Which was their usual practice when getting home from the bakery after a long day of work. Either that or having leftover bread or buns and jam. Either way, they rarely actually cooked a full meal for anything other than holidays.

"That sounds good. I wouldn't mind something other than frozen pasta or casserole," Erin admitted. She didn't normally go out for burgers, but they sounded awfully good after a steady diet of muffins, sandwiches, and frozen dinners.

"We're doing it then. We can either get something at the hospital cafeteria or hit a fast food restaurant on the way home."

"The hospital cafeteria isn't actually too bad. And that will keep the car from smelling like french fries for a week."

Vic grinned. They reached the door to Jeremy's room and Vic looked in to see whether he was alone. Sometimes when they arrived, the doctor or a nurse was there tending to his bandages or checking out his healing bullet holes. Vic stopped in the doorway, frozen. Erin couldn't see past her to see what was going on inside. Her heart started thumping hard in her chest.

"Vic?" she murmured. "What's up?"

Vic still didn't move or say anything. Then there was another voice that Erin didn't recognize.

"Well, look who's here!"

She could have mistaken it for Jeremy's voice, except that it was a bit huskier, and he didn't quite have the same cheeriness that Jeremy usually exuded.

"It's James," the voice went on. "The brother who ain't a brother."

Erin moved to try to see into the room. Vic finally seemed to break free of the paralysis that held her there.

"Joseph."

Vic moved into the room toward her older brother. Then Erin could see him. A man quite similar to Jeremy in looks, but broader and older, without Jeremy's laughing expression. Vic approached him and held her hand out stiffly, not hugging him as she would have Jeremy.

"Hi, how are you doing?"

Joseph gave her hand a couple pumps. He slapped her shoulder with his other hand, looking away from Vic as though he were uncomfortable with her. "How's it going, little bro?"

Vic looked at Jeremy, her eyes hurt.

"Come on, Joseph," Jeremy said roughly. "How would you like it if she refused to call you by your name? I don't care how awkward you think it is. Just start. It will get easier."

## APPLE-ACHIAN TREASURE

Joseph was a little flushed. He looked at Vic again, not sure what to say to this.

"Vic," Jeremy said. "Just call her Vic."

Joseph cleared his throat. "I don't know," he said. "This is all just... I've never called you that before. It's just not your name."

"I was named James Victor when I was born," Vic reminded him. "So, you can't complain that it isn't really my name, even if you aren't comfortable with my gender identity. I am Vic."

"Okay," Joseph nodded slowly. "Vic. How are you, Vic?"

Vic nodded graciously, as if she hadn't had to prompt Joseph with the proper etiquette. "I'm right as rain. How about you?"

Joseph forced a smile. "I can't complain. You taking care of this old guy?" Joseph indicated Jeremy.

"Who are you calling old?" Jeremy shot back. "I could still beat you."

"Huh. Doubt it," Joseph disagreed. "You're looking pretty poorly."

Jeremy shifted, sitting himself up taller on the bed, drawing himself up to look bigger and stronger. "I'll be out of here in no time. The doctors are just being extra careful."

Vic nodded at the repartee between her brothers. "What've you been doing lately, Joe? Haven't heard anything from you."

"Been busy on the farm," Joseph said curtly. "You know how much work it takes to run the place."

Vic looked at Jeremy, who had informed her that the family was no longer running the farm at full capacity, but was merely keeping it running as a front for the Jackson clan. Jeremy shrugged and didn't challenge Joseph.

"Which one of you was it I saw in Bald Eagle Falls a few weeks ago?" Erin asked. "Back when one of you was at the bakery. Before it burned down. Was that you?"

Joseph looked at her, his expression veiled. He wasn't about to give away whether it had been him or not.

"I didn't burn down anything."

"I didn't say you had. I just asked whether it was you I saw. You didn't exactly stay around to talk."

Joseph clearly wasn't about to be drawn into admitting it was him. Erin and Vic had avoiding discussing the fact that it might have been one of her own brothers who had burned down the bakery. Erin didn't want to make Vic feel any worse than she already did about her family situation and what had happened to Auntie Clem's Bakery, but they both knew in the backs of their minds that since one of the brothers had been seen there before the fire, it was probably one of them who had set it. Terry had questioned both brothers, but they had denied being in Bald Eagle Falls or having anything to do with the fire. Erin hadn't gotten a good enough look say which of them it had been.

"I'm just here visiting my brother," Joseph said, gesturing toward Jeremy. "I didn't come here to get into it again with you two about the bakery."

"Get into it again?" Vic repeated in disbelief. "Neither one of us has ever talked to you about the bakery. Don't make it sound like we've been throwing accusations around."

"Maybe you haven't talked to us about it, but that doesn't mean no one has. The cops have been around enough times, and don't think I don't know that it was you two who set them on us." Joseph nodded toward Erin. "It's your boyfriend who's the town cop, right? You can just tell him you were mistaken and to stay out of my business. He's a cop in Bald Eagle Falls, not in Moose River. He's got no jurisdiction out there."

Erin just looked at him.

"You guys just leave Vic and Erin alone," Jeremy told Joseph. "They're family, and you shouldn't be doing anything against family."

"They're not family," Joseph said slowly. "James—Vic decided that when he—she—decided to leave the family and to become…" he motioned widely to Vic's body and went on, uncomfortable. "And I don't know whether the two of you are an item," he included Vic and Erin both in his gesture this time, "but even if you are, that still doesn't make Erin Price family when James—Vic—isn't anymore." He scowled at Jeremy. "They're not family. So, I don't know why you're trying to protect them. If they don't want bad things to happen," he paused, letting Erin think about the bakery burning down, "then maybe you ought to stay out of the way of the clan."

"Staying out of the way of the clan isn't any guarantee of bad things not happening," Vic said. "Just ask Jeremy. He gets an honest job, and what happens? He gets shot by poachers."

Joseph gave an amused grin, his body language loosening a bit. "Well, that ain't nothin' to do with me. I can't help what other people do."

They all stood around for a minute, saying nothing, stuck in an awkward moment where there didn't seem to be anything appropriate to say.

"Well…" Joseph brushed his hands as if they were sandy. "I just came to see how my little brother was doing. I'll tell Mom that you're still in one piece."

"Say 'hi' for me," Jeremy agreed. "I'll be okay. She doesn't need to worry."

Joseph looked at Vic.

"I won't ask you to say 'hi' for me," Vic said slowly. "Since that would just cause more trouble than it's worth. She knows how to find me if she wants to talk. Until then… I guess she'll just have to be in the dark. I love you guys… but things are pretty screwed up right now."

The three looked at each other. Erin remembered a phrase that she'd heard used to describe the revolutionary war, about how 'brother fought against brother' and thought it apt. The three wanted so badly to just be family and be friends with each other again, but prejudices and criminal activities were keeping them apart.

They had once been so close, working and playing together. Erin could picture them all gathered together around the kitchen table, breaking bread together, maybe with a word of prayer or their pa reading a scripture to them. They had once been united, all working together. But circumstances had twisted everything apart, leaving them broken and unsure how to pick up the pieces.

"I guess I'll see you around," Joseph finally said to Jeremy. He punched him lightly on the shoulder. "Watch out for flying bullets."

He looked at Vic, then walked out without saying anything else to her.

# Chapter Nineteen

When Beaver arrived, Vic was sitting on the edge of Jeremy's bed, still looking stricken after her encounter with Joseph, in spite of Jeremy's and Erin's attempts to cheer her up again. It had been a long day, and Erin figured Vic was just too tired to bounce back. She would feel better in the morning.

Beaver looked at the glum faces and raised her eyebrows.

"You'd think I was walking into a funeral," she observed. "Was there bad news? Did the doctor say Jeremy only has a few more hours to live?"

Jeremy rolled his eyes at her. He squeezed Vic's hand and let it go again. "Joseph stopped by for a visit," he said. "It was just a little rough on Vic."

Beaver dropped into a visitor's chair, chewing on her gum. "Why?"

Erin looked for a way to answer and steer the conversation in another direction. Vic didn't need to keep going over the same ground. Jeremy too seemed to be trying to tell Beaver not to pursue it, shaking his head at her. "Nothing. It's fine. How was your day?"

"Joseph is a bully," Beaver said, not to be dissuaded. She kept her eyes on Vic. "Those boys know that turning you out on the street wasn't right, and that shunning you isn't right. But they're being indoctrinated and that's not something that is easy to break free from."

Vic looked at Beaver, her brows drawn down. "How do you know all of that? From Jeremy?" She turned her head to look at her brother.

He gave a self-conscious shrug, looking down at his hands. His normally ebullient manner was muted. "We talk," he admitted. "And Ro hears things through work."

"About Joseph? They aren't into drugs, are they? I don't want to hear that they're part of this drug trade."

Beaver didn't give any indication.

"I know Joseph was being a jerk," Jeremy said to Vic. "But she's right, they're being told all the time what to do and what to think. That kind of... brainwashing gets under your skin and into your brain. They want to do what's right, but it keeps getting twisted around."

"But *you* didn't turn out that way," Erin pointed out. "You've been really good to Vic. You came last Christmas and you came this summer when you thought she might be in danger. You treated her better than that."

"I wasn't there as long either. And me and James—Vic were closer. We were the two youngest, so we did everything together. The others were older, and they didn't really want their annoying little brothers getting underfoot all the time. So... we were closer to each other than Joseph and Daniel were to us."

"They're responsible for their own choices," Beaver said. "But they're older now, they've had to prove themselves to the clan, which means they've had to do some pretty bad stuff. And once you've got that on your conscience, it's easier to just believe the party line that what you're doing isn't really wrong. You go all in, because it's safer and feels better. You want to either be all in or all out."

Erin looked at Jeremy. "And you decided it was time to get out, before you... had to prove yourself."

Jeremy nodded. "I just... I dunno. I'm kind of a baby, you know. I've always had a soft heart. And that's not so

## APPLE-ACHIAN TREASURE

good when you're dealing with a group like the Jackson clan. Those people have to be rooted out."

Beaver nodded. "A soft heart is a liability. If you can't break someone of it, you've got to get them out some other way."

Jeremy shrugged. Vic touched his arm, nodding.

"In the rest of the world, it's not such a bad thing to have a soft heart."

"The world still thinks that a man should be macho and not cry at chick flicks. But it's getting better. I feel... more free now that I'm away from the family. While I was there, I felt like that was the only way to be, and that was the only place I'd ever belong. But it wasn't really true. That's just want they wanted me to think."

There was silence for a few minutes while everyone pondered this.

"Do you know about everyone in Bald Eagle Falls?" Erin asked Beaver, "or everyone who is from Bald Eagle Falls?" She was thinking about Beaver knowing details about Mary Lou's son Campbell.

"How could I?" Beaver laughed.

"It's not that big a place. It just seems like... you know about everyone, even people who aren't connected to your job. To drugs and whatever else you investigate."

"I'm not snooping into everyone's backgrounds, if that's what you're asking. We're not allowed to just investigate anyone without a reason. There has to be a reason to start looking at someone. You can't just look up your boyfriend's boss or sister because you're curious."

That somehow made Erin feel more uneasy instead of less. "So you would need to have reason to think that we were doing something illegal before you could look into our records?"

Beaver studied Erin, one corner of her mouth quirked into a smile. "Do you have something in your past that you would rather keep quiet, Erin Price?"

Erin looked at Beaver, her stomach tight and a little nauseated. She did have a past, and she didn't want anyone who felt like it digging into it to find out where she had come from and what she had done in her life.

"Doesn't everyone?" she asked, forcing bravado.

Beaver chuckled. She looked at Vic, who turned red.

"Okay, so I don't exactly like the idea of anyone investigating me, either," Vic admitted. "Everyone makes mistakes. No one wants people looking into their past and judging them by what they've done in the past." She looked at Jeremy, as if challenging him to ask what she could possibly have to be worried about. Jeremy didn't say anything. "I ran away. I was on my own. And there's not a lot of ways for an eighteen-year-old to make it on the streets alone without breaking a law or two. Erin knows I was down and out. I was squatting in the bakery. I didn't know where else to go. And yeah, I might have helped myself to something to eat or drink, and I know I wasn't supposed to be in the bakery, even if I did have a key. I mean, the key wasn't exactly mine, and Erin had no idea that I had it. She hadn't given me permission."

"I've never blamed you for any of that," Erin reminded her. "I know what it's like. I remember having to take care of myself when I didn't have anything."

"Vic…" Beaver shook her head, losing some of her amused demeanor for once. "I'm not investigating you. I'm just teasing. I told you, I can't just investigate anyone I feel like. If I did want to look into your past, I'd have to have a reason. A good one. I really don't think you need to worry that someone is going to slap you into jail for stealing a loaf of bread when you were out on the street."

Vic shrugged uncomfortably. "I'm not proud of everything I've done. I haven't always made good choices." She looked over at Jeremy. "Nobody makes good choices all of the time."

"No."

## APPLE-ACHIAN TREASURE

"So, when are you getting out of here?" Beaver demanded, changing the subject abruptly at the same time as she crossed one leg over the other and spread out to command as much space as possible. "Aren't those doctors tired of you yet?"

Vic nodded. "They must be. I can't imagine having this guy underfoot for more than a few days."

"They're promising me another day or two," Jeremy said. "If they change their minds, I might just have to check myself out anyway. It's really not much fun just sitting around here all day long. I want to be home. In my own space and able to sleep in my own bed instead of this thing, and not to have to listen to pages over the public address system and people walking up and down the halls at all hours or screaming that they want painkillers. It's bedlam."

"You'll be out before long," Vic assured him. "Just stick it out for a day or two longer until they say it's safe to leave."

"I'm with Jer," Beaver said. "I don't think I've ever stayed as long as the doctors wanted me to. You don't want to end up with some hospital infection and have them talking about wanting to cut off an arm or leg because of it. That's just… annoying."

Erin couldn't help laughing. Vic and Jeremy were smiling too.

"How many times *have* you been shot?" Erin asked.

Beaver shrugged her shoulders. "I wouldn't want to say. You know that most federal agents go through their entire careers without ever having to draw their weapon or be injured? Their whole careers."

"How long are those careers?" Jeremy asked.

"Well, that's a good question. I mean, if you decide it's not for you after a year or two, that's different from an agent who's been in for thirty or forty years."

"Do you know anyone who's been in for thirty or forty years?"

Beaver pursed her lips. "No, can't say I do. I don't know how long our director has been in… maybe he has… but I think they all move on to other things after a decade or two." She shook her head. "How about your new adventure? Any closer to getting that treasure?"

Erin looked at Vic, wondering if she should say anything. Vic shrugged and nodded. Erin started in on the latest details about Orson and his unexplained wealth. Beaver's eyes were alive with interest.

"Were you able to find any mines?"

Erin took out her phone and brought up the pictures they had taken at the farm. Beaver flicked through them.

"Well, well, well. Maybe Orson was getting more out of the ground than potatoes. When are you going to go down?"

"I don't know." Erin received her phone back from Beaver. "*I'm* not going down there. Vic is going to talk to Willie about getting the equipment they'll need and having a look. We won't be able to get back there for a few days, and we don't know what kind of shape the mines are going to be in. They haven't been maintained, so it might be a lot of work before we can find anything. If there's anything to be found."

# Chapter Twenty

ERIN HADN'T ACTUALLY TAKEN a shift with Charley before, so having Vic leave after lunch and Charley take over was a strange feeling. She wasn't exactly worried about it, but wasn't sure how they would get along together and whether it was going to be awkward the whole time Charley was there.

Erin tried to push aside any doubts and to pretend that Charley was just one of her other employees, someone who needed to be taught and trained but was perfectly competent and able to take it all on. She didn't need to worry about whether Charley was her boss or her partner, she just needed to show her the ropes. Erin was the one with experience, so she was the one who needed to show Charley how it was all done.

After the initial awkwardness, they had fallen into a rhythm. Not like the rhythm that Erin had with Vic, but she couldn't exactly expect that the first day, either.

"Here come some more," Charley advised.

Erin looked up from the display glass she was polishing to see the Fosters coming up to the door of the bakery. She gave them a big smile. "Well, here's my favorite customer. How is everybody?"

Mrs. Foster smiled and murmured a greeting while the children hurried forward to have a look at what was in the display case and negotiate what they were going to get. "Charley, this is the Foster family. Mrs. Foster with her son

Peter, and Karen, Jody, and Traci. Peter is very sensitive to gluten and is one of my best missionaries. He is always telling his friends that they should come here."

"Sometimes I think we single-handedly keep this place afloat," Mrs. Foster sighed, giving a tired smile. "Considering the number of times a week I am in here and the amount I walk away with."

"Well, we surely appreciate your business," Charley said, nodding graciously. "We couldn't do it without our customers."

"Erin has been so good to us. It's been amazing for Peter to actually have choices, instead of me having to run into the city to pick up a box of factory-produced cookies. He can have all kinds of wonderful baking that he wasn't able to touch before."

Charley nodded.

"Charley is my partner in the bakery now," Erin explained, though Mrs. Foster probably already knew all of the details. "She's the one who helped me to get the bakery going again after the fire. I couldn't have reopened without her."

Charley actually blushed. Erin laughed at her pink flush.

"And she's my half-sister too, but we never knew each other growing up, so we're still getting to know each other."

"You two look alike," Mrs. Foster agreed, looking from one to the other. "I can see the family resemblance. How nice for you to find each other. You don't have any other siblings, do you?"

"No. I grew up with a lot of different families, so I did grow up with brothers and sisters... but none of them were my own blood, and they came and went. I don't keep in close contact with any of them." She thought about Reg's visit and the odd phone calls that she occasionally got from the woman. She worried sometimes about what was going on with Reg. Erin shook off this stray thought. "Anyway, I'm really grateful for Charley. She came into my life at just the right time and really helped me to get back on my feet again."

Charley got pinker still. Erin laughed and looked down at the children.

"So, have you decided what you want?"

"Could we have one of the chocolate chip cookies?" Peter pointed at them. "And one of the ginger cookies. And…" he looked at Jody, "the banana bread? Is that what you want?"

Jody nodded. "I like banana bread," she told Erin, looking down at the loaf of bread in the display case.

"I do too," Erin confessed. "And I like to think they're better for you than the cookies. Less sugar, and the good vitamins and fiber from the banana."

"Know what I like better?"

"What?"

"Pumpkin bread."

"Oooh," Erin nodded. "I'll have to make sure I make some when pumpkins start showing up at the store for Halloween. I love pumpkin bread too."

Erin started to get out the treats for the children. She looked at Mrs. Foster. "And do you know what you want today?"

Mrs. Foster tried to keep Traci from getting her fingers all over the display case. "I'll need some sandwich bread for school lunches. And maybe some biscuits to go with the soup tonight. Do you need anything else, Peter?"

"Breakfast," Peter contributed. "Could I have bagels or muffins?"

"Why don't you just have cereal?"

Peter gave a martyred sigh. "I like muffins and bagels."

Mrs. Foster rolled her eyes. "Fine, then. One or the other, not both."

Peter looked into the display case. "Could I have… the bagels, then. Six?" he looked at his mother for confirmation.

"You make them last all week. No more than one per day."

"Okay."

Erin nodded. "Six bagels for Master Peter."

She packaged up the bagels and handed them over to Charley to ring through the till. Charley didn't take them. Her eyes were on the door. Erin looked to see who was there. It was a woman she didn't recognize. Middle-aged, dark hair, pleasant face. Her eyes were on Charley. Erin looked expectantly at Charley, waiting to be introduced. The woman entered and approached them.

"Hello, Charlotte," she said, prompting Charley to wake up and greet her.

"Uh... hi, Mom."

Erin blinked. Charley's mother? She nudged Charley aside to ring through the transaction and handed the baking to Mrs. Foster. Charley was still standing there like she didn't know what to do or say.

"Hi!" Erin said, holding out her hand to Charley's mother. "I'm Erin Price."

Mrs. Campbell smiled and shook Erin's hand. "Pleased to meet you, Erin."

"I'm Charley's half-sister. Biological."

Surprise registered on the woman's face. "Charley's sister?"

Erin glanced over at Charley. She had apparently not bothered to tell her mother about the discovery of her biological sister. Erin had thought that this would be big news, something that Charley would share with her family.

"Uh... yeah," Charley agreed weakly. "Um... surprise!"

Mrs. Campbell looked at the two of them, making the usual comparison of their features. "There is a resemblance," she admitted. "Have you actually done testing to see if you are?"

"Well, no. But Charley's birth date and information all match up."

## APPLE-ACHIAN TREASURE

"We were told that Charley was an only child. There were no siblings."

Erin shrugged uncomfortably. "There were a lot of things said and done at the time that weren't exactly ethical. I was told that my parents had died instantly in the accident, and they both lived for some months afterward. I was never told about Charley. I didn't find out about her being born until I requested my DHS records."

"That all seems very... unlikely."

"You can look at them if you want to. Charley is my mother's daughter. And she did have a DNA test to prove that she was Adam Plaint's daughter. She..." Erin made a motion to include her surroundings. "She inherited this place. So then we went into business together..."

She was probably saying too much. Wasn't it up to Charley to tell her own family about everything she had discovered? Erin didn't really know much about their relationship. Maybe Charley didn't want her family to know anything at all about Erin's mother and Adam Plaint. Erin looked over at Charley, who was still standing there looking thunderstruck that her mother had shown up in her bakery without any warning.

"Charley... do you want to show you mom around or offer her a free muffin?"

"What are you doing here?" Charley finally managed to ask.

"I came to see you. I don't understand why you didn't come home. If you finally decided not to have anything to do with that awful gang, then why didn't you come back home? And why all of the secrecy about this?" She pointed to Erin.

"I just want to live my own life. You don't control me. I can make my own decisions and go wherever I want."

"Clearly," Charley's mother agreed.

"I didn't want to come home like a boomerang kid. You guys don't need that. There's no reason you should have to support me when I'm an adult. I can take care of myself."

"You don't have to do it all on your own. We'd be happy to help. You know that. We've called. We've left messages. I don't know what else to do to convince you that we just want to be a part of your life. Don't cut us out."

Charley's expression was uncertain. She looked at Erin, then back at her mother.

"I think I should check on those cookies," Erin offered, turning to retreat to the kitchen to give them a chance to sort things out without an outsider listening in on their private conversation.

"No," Charley caught her by the sleeve. "I don't want you to leave. It's okay. I'm trying to figure this out. I don't know what to do."

"Well..." Erin looked at Mrs. Campbell and shrugged. "Don't you want your parents to be a part of your life? Just because you're working here and we've reconnected, that doesn't mean that you can't still be part of your family too. If they want to keep in touch..."

Erin didn't say how much she wished she had a family of her own to connect with. It would be so nice to be able to call up parents whenever she got lonely, to have plans with them for Christmas, to have someone to talk to when she was anxious, who was older and wiser and could give her advice. She had friends, but she would have given anything to have a family like Charley did too.

Maybe Charley sensed some of that. She looked away from her mother, biting her lip. "I should have called you back. I'm sorry. I've been sort of a brat. I know you still want to stay in touch."

"You know that the problem we had wasn't with you, it was with the choices that you were making. The people you were hanging around with. But this is nice. You've really turned things around. That makes me proud."

## APPLE-ACHIAN TREASURE

"You didn't come see me when I was in jail."

Mrs. Campbell didn't have any answer to that immediately. She looked into the display case at the various baked treats.

"I don't know what to say, Charlotte. You're the one who didn't want anything to do with us. And you expect us to swoop in the moment you get arrested? We told you that your lifestyle was going to get you in trouble. You pursued it anyway. You suffered the consequences. We couldn't change those consequences. That was something you had to deal with yourself."

"You could still have visited."

"I'm sorry that hurt your feelings. I hope you'll think about how we felt, hearing that you had murdered someone. That everything we had told you was going to happen did. We didn't know what to do or how we would be received if we did try to visit you. You are the one who broke off contact with us and made it clear that you didn't want us to be a part of your life."

"I know."

Erin stared into the display case, hot and uncomfortable. "How about a free muffin?"

Charley and her mother looked at Erin, brows drawn down, their movements mirrors of each other. Charley spread her hands out.

"Why not a muffin?" She said. "Do you want a muffin, Mom?"

Mrs. Campbell pointed to one of the chocolate chip ones. "I know I should probably go with a bran muffin, but those look so good."

Erin got one out and handed it across to her in a napkin. "They *are* really good."

"So, this is a specialty bakery?" Mrs. Campbell looked around. "You have a section that is gluten-free?"

"Everything is gluten-free," Erin informed Mrs. Campbell as she bit into the muffin, rolling her eyes at the moist muffin studded with chocolate chips.

"This is gluten-free?"

"Yes. Everything."

"How do you do that? Do you have a special kind of flour?"

"Most of them are combinations of flours," Charley jumped in, eager to impart what she had been learning. "There isn't one gluten-free flour that can substitute satisfactorily for wheat or other gluten flours. You need a few different ones to mimic the properties of wheat flour."

"Why did you name it Auntie Clem's? Couldn't you name it after one of your real aunties?"

"Oh, that's me," Erin explained. "I operated the bakery across the street before it burned down. Charley helped me get back on my feet, and I helped her open the bakery. She wanted to keep the name of Auntie Clem's because it had a good reputation. People knew what it was and what we offered already."

"You could have named it something else," Mrs. Campbell asserted, looking at Charley.

"I know I could. But that's what I wanted. There's nothing wrong with it."

"No, of course not," Mrs. Campbell said.

"I wanted Erin on board, and I wanted her goodwill. So I used her name. It's sound business practices."

Erin looked again toward the kitchen and the fictional burning cookies. She really didn't want to stay there and listen to Charley and her mother bickering. Some people enjoyed getting into arguments or watching other people's arguments. Erin was not one of them. She was an avoider, through and through. She did whatever she could to avoid getting in the middle of an argument, especially somebody else's argument.

## APPLE-ACHIAN TREASURE

"Are you going to be in town for a while?" Charley asked her mother, looking at the clock on the wall. "We could get together for dinner before you go home, if you want to talk. If you really want to visit," she added, "and not just criticize."

"Of course I do! I would love to get together for dinner. Why don't you come home and we could have dinner there?"

"Mom… I've got work. I don't have time to drive out to Moose River, have supper, and then drive back. If you want to stick around for a little while, I'll join you when I'm done here. Otherwise, we can set up another day."

"And you'll answer the phone?"

Charley rolled her eyes. "I'll answer the phone."

"What time are you off?"

"We close at five, and then I need to help with the cleanup and tomorrow's prep—"

"I can do that without you today," Erin said. "It won't take up that much time. Then your mom can still get back to Moose River before it's really late."

Charley shot Erin a look, then gave a grudging nod. "Does that work?"

Mrs. Campbell nodded. She smiled at them both. "How lovely. I'm so looking forward to it. Thank you for being so generous, Erin. And thank you for the muffin. They really are fantastic."

Erin nodded. "You're welcome. Come again."

Mrs. Campbell waved and left the bakery. Erin forced a smile at Charley. Charley put her face in her hands, clearly not happy.

"What have I done now?"

## Chapter Twenty-One

WILLIE ROLLED UP TO the house and honked the horn. When Erin and Vic didn't immediately join him at the truck, he locked it up and went up to the house. He knocked on the door and tried the handle. It was unlocked, so he went in.

"You girls ready to go?" he asked, looking through to the kitchen.

"Just about," Vic promised. "We're just finishing up on some sandwiches. We'll be well-supplied."

"You didn't need to make anything," Willie said. "We could have just picked something up on the way."

"I wanted to contribute something," Erin explained. "I don't have any caving equipment or expertise, but I can do sandwiches! This way we won't have to stop for food, and we'll have enough that we don't have to stop if you guys are into something and want to keep working."

Willie walked into the kitchen and helped himself to a slice of bacon before Vic could stop him. She tried to slap his hand, but missed. Willie shoved the bacon into his mouth, grinning.

"Okay, I approve."

"I'm still worried about this," Erin confessed. "What if something happens…? I don't want you to get trapped underground."

"No one is going to get trapped," Willie assured her. "I spend half my life underground. I know what I'm doing."

# APPLE-ACHIAN TREASURE

"But this mine is old. We don't know what kind of condition it is going to be in."

"That's why I'm going to have a look," Willie said patiently. "I'm not going to go in if it's unsafe. If we need to shore up the walls, we can get started on that. If it's collapsed, then we can take a look around and see if there is another way to go in. I'm not going to just rush into a mine without being absolutely sure that it's safe."

"But something could happen."

"No. Nothing is going to happen."

"That time before, you got hurt. You hit your head, and there was a pool of blood, and we were so worried about you."

Willie held her gaze. His face was perfectly calm. "Erin. You know I didn't just happen to bump my head. Somebody helped me along. And I'm not going to be alone today. Vic is going to come. Jeremy is going to come. None of us are going to be alone. You're welcome to come along too, if you like."

"No way," Erin said. "There is no way you're getting me underground."

"You go downstairs. It's really no different. It's perfectly safe. I'm not going to take Vic or you anywhere that I think there is any danger of either of you getting hurt. It wouldn't be anything like when you were underground before. We'll all be working together and helping each other out."

"I'm not going," Erin maintained. "I'll stay outside and then I can call for trouble if anything happens."

"Nothing is going to—"

"I know. But I'm going to be there just in case. Besides, whenever you have someone there in case of an emergency, you end up not needing them, right? So as long as I'm there watching for trouble, there won't be any."

Willie sighed and shook his head at Vic. Vic rolled her eyes and shrugged with one shoulder. "You're not going to convince her," she said. "I've done my best. But Erin has already had a couple of negative experiences. It's not because she just doesn't like tight spaces."

Erin shuddered. She started wrapping the sandwiches they had made, neatly tearing the plastic wrap off of the industrial-size roll, wrapping the sandwiches tightly and stacking them to the side. Willie watched her.

"You're not a coward," he told her.

Erin looked at him, her face getting warm. "I sort of am," she said. "I could try to go into the mine with you. I'd have an expert right there on hand. I know in my head that nothing could happen to me down there with you right there. But I don't even want to try. I just want to wrap a blanket around myself and wait for you to come back out."

"That's okay. Vic is right, you do have good reason for not wanting to go down there. That doesn't make you a coward. You are a brave person."

Erin shrugged. "Eh. Doesn't matter. Results are the same."

As Erin wrapped, Willie started to fill the cooler that was on hand. Erin added some boxes of juice from the fridge, napkins, cookies, cut up fruit and veggies.

Willie shook his head. "All of this for one day? It's a feast."

"I know how much you guys eat. There's not going to be much left over. Especially if we end up covering for two meals. You guys will be like the plague of locusts."

"I don't know. This looks like a lot."

"When you're hungry it won't be. Especially with Jeremy along."

They were finally finished getting everything packed. Willie waited impatiently for a couple more minutes while Erin and Vic gave the animals their treats and said their goodbyes.

"You're going to be back tonight," he pointed out. "It isn't like you're going away for a week."

## APPLE-ACHIAN TREASURE

"We'll be back," Erin agreed. She scratched Marshmallow's ears. "Don't you go getting getting into any trouble." She shook her head. "He's has been crazy lately. He's been getting into the houseplants, chewing on the legs of the couch... I don't know what to think. He's always been so well-behaved before."

"I'm sure he'll be fine without you for a few hours."

"I know." Erin said goodbye to Orange Blossom, and then they were on their way. Willie led them out to the truck. He went around to the driver's side. When he looked at Vic, she hadn't climbed into the car, but was standing outside looking down.

"Vic. What's up?"

"No, it's what's down," Vic said.

Willie walked back around the car and looked down at the tire. It was completely flat.

Willie swore. He replayed the trip over to Erin's house back in his mind and shook his head. It had been a perfectly smooth ride with no issues. Which meant that it had somehow gone from fully inflated to completely flat in the twenty minutes or so he had been in the house trying to get Erin and Vic on their way.

"You must have driven over a nail," Vic said, studying what she could see of the tread for the head of a nail.

"Must have," Willie agreed. He went to the back of the truck and moved things around in order to get out his jack and spare tire and the rest of the tools that he needed. Erin stood by feeling useless while Vic and Willie quickly swapped out the flat tire. While Willie put on the spare, Vic was rolling the flat, looking for some sign of why it had gone flat.

When Willie was finished, he went over to look at the tire. "Find anything?"

Vic turned it around and pointed to the wall of the tire. Willie leaned in. Vic pressed her thumb to the sidewall and

Willie saw the small slit open up. He looked at Vic, his brows drawing down. "Somebody slashed my tire?"

Vic nodded.

Erin got closer to have a look, though she was certainly no expert on sabotage to tires. She saw the short, straight slit in the tire. "Couldn't it just have popped or burst? It could just be an accident, right?"

"No," Willie shook his head. "I don't think so. That looks intentional."

"But who would slash your tire?"

Willie walked around the truck, looking at the others. If some unknown party had slashed one of his tires, Willie was lucky he hadn't slashed all four of them. Maybe he had been interrupted. Or maybe the perp had just chickened out and couldn't do more than one. At least where it was only one tire, they could fix it immediately and get back on the road.

"There are plenty of people around Bald Eagle Falls who don't particularly like me," he admitted. "I would think that most of them wouldn't care anymore. It isn't like I'm getting in anyone's way. I would think that anyone who planned to do anything would have done so years ago."

"You haven't started anything recently that someone might be upset with you about?" Vic asked.

Willie shook his head. "No, nothing new."

"Then do you think…" Vic trailed off.

Willie looked at her. "What?"

"I just wondered if you think it's because someone doesn't want us going to Orson's mine. Maybe this is a warning to stay away. Or an attempt to get us to stop so they can get there ahead of us…"

Willie let out his breath in a thin stream. "I don't think anyone really cares that much about this treasure hunt," he said slowly. "Although…"

"Erin got hit over the head for the maps and poem," Vic filled in. "So, we know that *someone* is taking an interest. Someone who maybe followed us all the way from Bald

## APPLE-ACHIAN TREASURE

Eagle Falls to the hospital. And then stuck around for hours to see you give Erin the maps."

Willie nodded slowly. Erin didn't like the idea. "Maybe we shouldn't go, then. Maybe it's too dangerous. I don't want anyone to get hurt."

Willie loaded the damaged tire into the back of the truck, then put away his tools. He looked at Erin, his face a mask. "I don't think you need to worry about it. If they really wanted to keep me from the mine, they'd know that they had to do a lot more than just puncture one tire. Anyone who knows me knows that I'm handy and that I've got all the tools I need right here in the truck. There's no point in just flattening one tire."

"So you don't think it was intentional."

"Maybe it was, maybe it wasn't. But they didn't flatten all four, which is what they'd really need to do to slow us down for any length of time. Then I'd need a tow and four new tires before I could get on the road. Just slashing one tire… More likely someone who just has a grudge. Doesn't like something I've been doing lately. I don't know who or why. I'll have to think about it."

"Maybe we shouldn't go to the mine today. Then you have a few days to think about it and investigate properly…"

Willie motioned to the truck. "Hop in. I'm not letting this stop me."

Vic got in as instructed. Willie went around to the driver's door again and got in. Erin was the only one left standing on the sidewalk, dithering about whether it was the right thing to do.

"Get in, Erin," Vic urged. "Come on. We're going. We'll pick up Jeremy and between all of us, we'll be just fine. No one is going to come after all of us."

Erin was still uneasy when they got to Orson's farm. But Vic and Jeremy were talking and laughing as if nothing had happened, and Willie didn't seem to be overly concerned about who might have tried to sabotage his truck. No one acted like it was a big deal.

Willie was a lot faster going over the old roads than Vic had been, and a couple of times they overshot a turn. Erin felt rattled to pieces when they got there and was glad to get out of the truck.

Willie got out and started to circle the truck and tramp back and forth over the area where they had parked, the same place that Vic and Erin had previously stopped to have a look around. He was looking down at the ground. Erin followed him.

"What are you looking for?"

"Just checking for any signs that anyone else has been here."

"And… has there been?"

"Impossible to tell." Willie shrugged. "If someone has been here, they didn't make it obvious. Everything is so overgrown, there's no way to know if they were trying to cover their tracks or if there just hasn't been anyone around. At any rate," Willie took a look around the farm, "it doesn't look like there's anyone here now. So why don't you show me the mine entrances. We'll have a look at their condition. That's what I'm here for, isn't it?"

Erin and Vic took the lead, taking Willie to the place they had taken pictures of the entrances to the mines. They too were overgrown, and Erin was sure that all of the supporting beams and structures had given way. It was way too dangerous for anyone to go into the mines in their current condition.

"Not bad," Willie said, which was not what Erin was hoping to hear. Willie pulled out a strong flashlight and shone it around the inside of the entrances. "It all looks pretty clear. Lots of solid rock, so it's held up pretty well."

He took a couple of steps inside.

"Do you really think you should do that?" Erin asked, her voice squeaking up. He had said that he wouldn't go inside. He'd said that he would just look at it. She wasn't ready for him to go in.

"I'm just right here, Erin," Willie assured, his voice close at hand. "I'm not doing anything dangerous. Just having a look at the condition."

"I don't think we're going to find anything in there. If there was anything to be found, then someone would have found it in the last hundred and fifty years. Even if Orson did hide the source of his treasure, it has long since been raided. People would have looked at the mines before anything else. Well, maybe the house first, but the mines would be the natural place for anyone to search for it."

"Don't freak out now," Vic advised. "Why don't you go sit down? If you don't look at the mines, maybe you'll be able to calm down."

Erin moved a short distance away and sat down, but it didn't make her feel better. Not with Willie already inside the mine, and Jeremy and Vic super close behind him, hanging around the tunnel entrances and talking and pointing and thumping the walls. Erin knew that it wouldn't be long before they all decided to go in.

## Chapter Twenty-Two

SHE WAS RIGHT. WITHIN the hour, Willie had brought over half the equipment in his truck. He was suiting up and showing Vic and Jeremy how to handle their equipment, even though Vic had been caving with him before. Erin bit her fingernails. She knew she didn't have any influence over them. If they wanted to go into the mine, they were going to go into the mine. And Erin couldn't control what would happen to them when they did, and neither could they. They could make the choice, but they couldn't choose the consequences.

"It will be fine, Erin," Vic said as she pulled a backpack on. "Willie says it's perfectly safe. Everything still looks strong. There aren't any loose beams or rocks or anything. Everything was built really well. It's in better shape than the house, and you went into the house."

At least if the house had collapsed on them, there would only have been a few boards coming down on their heads. Not half the mountain. They would have been able to push themselves out from beneath the debris. It wasn't the same with crawling into a mining tunnel. They could easily be hurt or killed if there was a cave-in and they ended up being hit, buried, or trapped by falling rock.

"I just don't have a good feeling about it," Erin said, shaking her head. She wished that she hadn't told anybody about the poem. She should have just read it and left it there in Clementine's papers. Clementine had known what she

## APPLE-ACHIAN TREASURE

was doing. Just put the poem in with the genealogy papers and leave it there as a bit of history. What had made Erin think that it was a good idea to go searching for hidden treasure? Why had she told Vic about it? She should have known that Vic would instantly want to pick up the adventure. She was always up for a bit of excitement.

"You don't have a good feeling because you're afraid of enclosed spaces," Vic pointed out. "It isn't anything to do with these particular mines. It's just a bad feeling because you had a couple of bad experiences. You can't let that stop you from enjoying life."

"I really don't think you should go in there," Erin insisted. She could feel tears welling up in her eyes, but she didn't care anymore. Let them see her tears. Maybe it would convince them that what they were doing really was dangerous and unnecessary. What did they think? That they were going to go walking into one of those mining tunnels and just find Orson's treasure, lying in the open? Other people had looked for the treasure. They weren't going to find it.

"Erin." Willie approached Erin. He gave her a hug. "It's going to be okay. You don't need to worry about us. If you want to come in, I'll show you. You can see that it's sturdily-built and there isn't any danger to us."

His arms felt good around her. For a minute, Erin just closed her eyes and reminded herself that she was safe. They were all perfectly safe in Willie's capable hands. She knew he was careful. He didn't rush into things. He knew how to handle himself in an emergency. Even if something did happen, Willie would be able to take care of it. He had always come to her rescue before.

"Don't go in there," she told him anyway.

"Do you want to see? I'll show you."

"No. Just don't go in."

He shook his head and gave her another squeeze before releasing her. "It's going to be okay; you'll see."

Erin couldn't help it. Tears escaped her eyes and she turned away from them, trying to find some mental space to get past the feelings of fear and dread.

She could hear Vic inquiring softly, questioning whether maybe they should just give it up if Erin felt so strongly about it. But Willie murmured that Erin would be okay and that she'd settle down once they were inside, and the little group went ahead.

Erin didn't say goodbye to them. She watched them enter the mine one at a time, just waiting for something to happen. But there wasn't a collapse the minute they walked into the mine. She could hear their voices, cheerful and excited, as they started to explore. She stayed near the entrance for a long time, until their voices had faded away. Nothing had happened. They were okay. Just like Willie had said, the mine tunnel was well-constructed and would probably last several hundred more years. Orson had known what he was doing.

They would explore the empty tunnels, see where Orson had dug looking for gold or whatever he had been mining for, and then they would be back out. Even though they had brought enough food for a couple of meals, they would only spend a couple of hours exploring the tunnels, and then decide that there wasn't anything down there. They would all pile back into the truck and go home.

Thinking about the truck, Erin went back to the vehicle to ensure that everything was still in order with it. She walked around it, checking out each of the tires. It was always possible that whoever had slashed the one tire had intended to do them all. He could easily have followed them there, and then once Willie and the others were in the mine, he could sabotage the rest of the tires and strand them.

But everything looked fine. The tires were all fully inflated and there were no other vehicles around. Birds were singing lustily in the trees. A light wind was blowing through the trees. Everything was calm and peaceful.

## APPLE-ACHIAN TREASURE

There was a muffled thud. Erin felt the ground beneath her feet give a shudder, and the birds stopped singing.

A plume of dust or smoke rose in the air.

# Chapter Twenty-Three

ERIN LOOKED AROUND. SHE wasn't sure what had just happened, but she knew something was wrong. She looked at the truck once more, worried that if someone had messed with it, they wouldn't be able to get back home. But the truck looked fine. Erin pulled out her phone and looked at it. She had no signal. She hadn't expected to have one, but it still made her anxious not to be able to reach out. How had Orson and the other farmers been able to live that way, totally out of touch with each other? No way to communicate unless they got on a horse—or their own two feet—and physically went to find the nearest neighbor. And maybe he would not be there, having gone into town or to some other destination.

During Erin's time, all of those neighbors had moved away, into the cities and other populated centers, leaving the old farms abandoned and isolated.

Erin walked back to the mine entrance. She walked closer to the entrance and listened for their voices.

"Vic? Willie? Is everything okay"

Her voice bounced back to her. Erin had a sick, tight feeling in her stomach. Something wasn't right. She wasn't sure what it was, but she knew there was a problem. What had happened?

"Vic?"

Willie had given Erin check-in times. If they took more than a few hours in the mine and didn't check in with her,

# APPLE-ACHIAN TREASURE

then she was to assume that something had happened and to call for help. She would not go into the mine after them, she would get in touch with someone who could do a proper search.

"Willie?"

There was no answer. Erin looked at her phone for the time. They had not been in there for long. It wasn't time for them to contact her. She went to the radio equipment Willie had left behind. It wouldn't work if they had gone down too deep into the ground, but Willie hadn't thought that the tunnels were very deep. Not like some of the caves that he had been in before.

Erin fiddled with the emergency radio. He had shown her how to use it, but everything he had said had gone straight out of Erin's mind. She turned the volume up and clicked the button on the microphone.

"Willie? Can you hear me?"

There was only crackling in response. Erin listened closely, trying to hear through the crackle for Willie's voice. She could just see him rolling his eyes at Vic and making a comment about how she couldn't go two minutes without assuming that something catastrophic had occurred. She waited for his reassuring voice, but couldn't hear anything.

"Willie? Are you there? Come in, please."

Still no response. Erin looked around. The birds were singing once more. A crow circled way up high in the sky up above her, and Erin was reminded of Skye, Adele's crow. He was so smart. Adele had said that crows were one of the smartest birds, approaching human intelligence.

"At least, we assume by the tests that we have done on them that they are *almost* as smart as humans," Adele remarked. "I happen to think that they may just be smarter. How would you test an animal to see if it was smarter than you? Humans only assume that they are the smartest species on the planet. But that's a little arrogant."

"Hey Skye," Erin said softly, looking up at the bird. Of course it wasn't Skye. It was another crow. But she was still encouraged to have the bird fly over her, feeling like she wasn't quite so alone.

"Willie. Vic. Jeremy. Come in, please."

She thought she might have heard a squawk back, but she couldn't make out any words. Erin clicked the mike button and released it. Where were they and why weren't they answering? They shouldn't already be so deep that Erin couldn't reach them.

Erin looked up at the sky at the crow again. What had he seen up there? Had he been able to feel the vibration that Erin had sensed through her feet? What had caused that?

"Willie?" Erin went back to the entrance of the mine and called him again. "Willie! Are you down there?"

No answer.

No sound from inside.

Erin looked at the equipment they had left behind. She put on a helmet with a light, picked up a bottle of water, and stepped into the entrance of the mine.

# Chapter Twenty-Four

THE ENTRANCE TUNNEL WAS broad, easy to walk through. Like a hallway. Erin could still see the light from the outside world. Everything was normal and looked perfectly safe. It wasn't like the caves where she had to crawl on her belly because of cramped quarters. But Erin knew it wouldn't be that wide all the way through. Before long, Orson would have figured out that it was too much work to keep cutting that wide of a tunnel through the rock. He only needed to cut it big enough to get himself and his equipment through.

Erin ignored the nausea and how fast her heart was beating. She couldn't afford to be sick and scared. Not if something had happened to her friends.

They hadn't been in there for long. If Erin moved at a quick pace, she would catch up to them. They would be moving slowly, admiring the tunnel and looking for clues. They would all laugh at how she had gone into the tunnel after all, when everything was perfectly fine.

Erin tried to call out to them, but she couldn't get the words out. Her throat was dry and hot and constricted. But she wasn't going to cry. They were going to be just fine. Willie had said so. Willie had said that the tunnel was perfectly safe.

She continued to press forward, trying not to think about the tunnel closing in around her. She was able to move and breathe freely. There was nothing to worry about. In a few minutes, if she kept moving at a brisk pace, she would be able to hear them and to call out to them to stop and wait for her. They would laugh at her being such a paranoid wimp, but she would at least know that they were safe, and she could return to the outside even if she couldn't convince them to return with her.

But in a couple more minutes, the tunnel ended. Erin looked around, disoriented. She turned a slow circle, letting her light shine in each direction, understanding that she must have missed a branch off into another direction. But the only tunnel she could find was the way she had come in. Erin turned again, studying each wall, looking at the way that it was carved out and the supporting beams were placed. She went suddenly cold, and it wasn't because she was underground and away from the sun.

One of the rock walls that she faced was not the same as the others. Rather than being carved out of the mine, it was filled with smaller pieces of rock. Like a giant had taken a handful of rocks and plugged it up.

Erin grabbed a couple of rocks and pulled them away. She threw them down and attacked the pile of rocks with vigor, calling out her friends' names. "Vic! Willie! Can you hear me? Jeremy? Are you there? I'm right here, can you hear me?"

She paused in her removal of the rocks, straining her ears for some sound. She couldn't hear any answering voices. What if something had happened to them? What if rather than just a cave-in of the tunnel blocking their way back, one of them had been hurt? Buried under the pile of rubble?

She worked more frantically, moving rock as quickly as she could, but she didn't seem to be making a dent in it. There could be a mile of debris to pick through, and she hadn't even made an appreciable dent in the edge she could see.

## APPLE-ACHIAN TREASURE

"Come on!" Erin tried to make herself move faster. But even as she tried to force herself, she couldn't help thinking about the logistics of the job. She couldn't just throw the rocks she cleared to the side. If she was able to move enough of the rock out of the way, she would just end up filling the tunnel behind her with rock They had to be transported out of the tunnel. And that would require equipment, which Erin didn't have. She stopped and looked at the problem, forcing herself to slow down and really think it through. Just attacking the fallen rocks by herself wasn't going to do anything for her friends. It was a hopeless venture. She had to get help.

Even though she hated to leave them behind and to stop the work on the fallen rocks, Erin forced herself to turn around and retreat down the tunnel. She tripped over a couple of the rocks that she had discarded along the way, making herself grimace at the mess she had left.

She hurried out to the radio equipment. Her eyes teared in the bright sunshine. She wiped away the moisture and picked up the radio mike again.

"Willie? Are you there? Can you hear me?"

She released the button and waited for a response. Her whole body was tense as she strained for an answer. She wanted so badly to hear some kind of response. Something to indicate that they were still alive and waiting for her. There was nothing. Erin's fingers moved of their own accord. She couldn't remember all of the steps that Willie had shown her, but her fingers changed the frequency to the emergency band and she pressed the button down again.

"Mayday, mayday. Is anybody listening?" Did people really say 'mayday' when they were calling for help? Or was that only boats? Would someone monitoring the frequency just laugh at her or think she was some kid fooling around?

Erin heard a response and tried to fine tune the frequency to make it clearer.

"Is somebody there? This is Erin Price."

The crackle she got back was clearer the second time. Erin could make out the words "emergency dispatcher." It had to be the woman who manned the phones back in Bald Eagle Falls, relaying messages to the police officers or volunteer fire department, or who made the decision when to contact emergency services in the city to have them send help.

"There's been a cave-in," Erin explained, tears filling her eyes and choking her throat. "We're on Orson Cadaver's old farm. There's a mine. There's been a cave-in."

"…everyone safe?"

"No." Erin swallowed hard and tried to go on. "There are three people trapped. I don't know if there are any injuries."

"Coordinates?"

"I don't know." Erin looked around her for some clue. She pulled out her phone and launched the map app. Would the GPS work when she couldn't get a phone signal? It looked like the flashing circle was in the right spot on the map, so Erin tapped it and read the coordinates to the dispatcher.

"Again?"

Erin read the numbers as slowly and clearly as possible.

"Once more?"

Erin read them again, feeling frustrated.

There was a burst of crackles. "…stay on this channel…"

Erin wanted to go back into the tunnel and remove more rocks from the caved-in area, but she knew she needed to do what she was told and relay whatever information the emergency responders might need. It would do more good to get the proper help there than it would to try to shift the pile of rocks by herself. But she wanted to do something more active, not to just sit there by the radio waiting for the next question.

# APPLE-ACHIAN TREASURE

The next voice she heard on the radio was one that sent a warm flush radiating from her heart to the top of her head and the tips of her toes.

"Erin?"

"Terry!"

"…what happened?"

"They went down the mine to look for the treasure or more clues. There was a noise… I went to look… can't get them on the radio… there's rock blocking the tunnel."

"Is Willie there?"

Erin nodded, wiping her nose. She took a minute to try to steady her voice before pressing the button on the mike to answer. "He's in the mine."

Whatever Terry had to say about that, he said offline, not into the radio. Erin didn't imagine it was anything that could be repeated in polite company.

Erin knew that Terry liked to call on Willie to help with rescue work or coordinate in an emergency. While it was good that Vic and Jeremy had an expert to help them, Terry could have done with another Willie on the outside to help with the rescue efforts.

"…on my way…" Terry's voice was coming from the radio again. "…be there soon…"

"Okay." Erin tried to hold the radio mike steady, aware that her hand was shaking. "See you then."

Then he was gone. Erin looked at the time on her phone. It would take an hour for Terry to get out to her. Maybe shorter if he used his lights and siren, but he wouldn't be able to get through the rough trails much faster than Willie had. And Terry wouldn't have a map showing where the roads were. Unless he had paper maps in the car to find his way around the old country roads. Hopefully, somebody had thought of that.

Mostly, Erin sat by the radio waiting for any contact from the dispatcher or Terry. Every now and then she went back into the mine to shout at the wall of rock, hoping to get a reply from the other side. How deep was the rock? Was there so much that it blocked out all of the sound, or had her friends been hurt or even killed in the collapse?

She had known it was too dangerous to go into the mine. Why hadn't anyone listened to her?

It seemed like a long time before she heard Terry's voice over the emergency band again.

"I'm at Willie's truck, Erin. Are you okay?"

Erin looked back toward where the truck was parked. She couldn't see either vehicle, but didn't doubt that Terry knew Willie's truck when he saw it.

"I'm okay."

"I'm going to be a couple of minutes while I unload his emergency gear. Hang tough."

"Okay."

She was glad to know that he was there. She could feel her heart rate slow and her muscles relax, knowing that the first help had arrived. They were going to need a lot more than just Terry, but at least he was there. It was a start.

Eventually, she could see Terry heading toward her, laden down with backpacks and bags, K9 at his side. Erin got to her feet to help him.

"What can I take?"

He shuffled his load to hand her a couple of first-aid bags. "Here, grab those."

The bags were probably the lightest thing he was carrying, but they were still heavy. Erin was glad for the muscle burn. Glad that she was finally doing something to help. They carried everything to the mine entrance and put them down.

"Has there been any more noise?" Terry asked. "Any more falling rocks?"

"I haven't heard anything."

"Have you been inside?"

## APPLE-ACHIAN TREASURE

"A few times. It doesn't seem like anything else is unstable."

"I'll take a look. Have you heard anything from them?"

"No. Nothing."

Terry looked grim, but didn't say anything negative. "I'm going to take a look at what we've got, and then we'll try to coordinate the rescue efforts. People in town are getting geared up. Some of them are already on their way."

Erin nodded, her throat hot and her eyes tearing up again. Terry gave her a brief hug. "We'll get them out. Don't cry."

"Why did I ever start this? It's my fault they're in there. If I hadn't started this silly treasure hunt, it never would have happened."

"You can't predict an accident like this. Willie checked it out before going in. If he couldn't tell there was a danger, no one could have. There is always a risk in a place like this, but he obviously didn't think there was anything too hazardous, or he wouldn't have gone in. He certainly never would have taken Vic in with him."

"They could be hurt."

He squeezed her arm. "I'm going in. I can't stop to talk about it."

Erin nodded. Terry turned on his helmet light and walked into the mine.

Even though Erin had been in and out several times since the collapse, she was nervous about him entering. What if there was another rockfall and he ended up getting hurt too?

The radio was squawking when Erin got back to it. She couldn't sort out all of the voices. It sounded like the volunteers were being organized, but it wasn't clear enough on Erin's end to be sure how many people were involved or what they were planning to do when they got there.

How were they going to move all of that rock?

Terry was out a few minutes later. He nodded at Erin.

"We're definitely going to need a hand in there. Do you have maps of the mining tunnels?"

"I do, but they're hard to follow. I don't think they're drawn to scale very well, and the landmarks are hard to see or have changed."

She got out the maps and she and Terry bent over them, following the faint lines.

"So, this is where we are?" Terry pointed.

Erin nodded. "Yeah."

"I want to know if there are any other tunnels that lead through to here," he tapped the map, indicating the area hopefully beyond the rockslide. If Willie, Vic, and Jeremy had been safely on the other side of the affected area, they might be uninjured, but their exit would be blocked until they found a way to get all of the rock out of there. There was so much of it, Erin was afraid they would be looking at weeks rather than hours or even days. How would they survive that long even if they were uninjured?

Erin looked for some sign of another way in. The lines were so faint, it was nearly impossible to tell where a tunnel ended and where the ink was just faded. There were a couple of tunnels that might have fed into the one that her friends were in, but she couldn't be sure.

# Chapter Twenty-Five

PERRY HAD GONE TO scout around with K9 to see how the other mine entrances looked before making any kind of decision as to how they were going to effect a rescue. If the other tunnels looked unstable, they would need engineers and heavy equipment before they could start anything. Erin was crossing her fingers and hoping that the other tunnels would look fine and they could try to get closer to Vic, Willie, and Jeremy from another direction. She sat babysitting the radio and answering questions whenever she could. Looking up, she saw Beaver coming through the woods toward her. She had a long, fluid walk that made Erin think of a wolf loping across the prairie. Erin gave her a little wave. Beaver looked surprised to see Erin there.

"Hey, how's it going, Erin?"

Erin looked at her. "Well, not so great."

Beaver's eyebrows went up. "What's up? I saw Officer Piper's truck go by, and it's parked down there. I thought I would find the two of you together, where did he go?"

"To see how the other mine entrances look." Erin motioned to the nearest entrance.

"Is he helping with the treasure hunting, then?"

Erin cleared her throat. She searched Beaver's expression for some sign that she knew what was going on, but Beaver's expression, as usual, was pleasant and amused. The emergency radio crackled to life, and Erin tried to understand what was being said. They were just confirming that they had called for help from the heavy equipment team in the city. Erin looked back at Beaver.

"There was a cave-in," she explained. "I guess you haven't heard."

"A cave-in," Beaver repeated. She blinked at Erin, then looked at the entrance to the mine. "Are you talking about right here? Now? Or back when the treasure was hidden…?"

"Now. Just through there." Erin pointed.

"Was there anyone in there?"

"Vic, Willie, and…" Erin had a hard time getting the painful news out. "Jeremy."

Beaver's face was pale. "Are they okay?"

"We haven't been able to get them. I don't know if it's just because of the rock or whether they were injured and can't answer."

Beaver folded to the ground beside Erin. "They're still in there? And you don't know whether or not they are hurt?"

Erin nodded. "Yeah."

Beaver sat there, staring at the entrance to the mine, her face pale and drawn. The usual smile was gone. She still chewed on her gum, but it was slow and uncertain instead of her usual chomping. Erin wondered whether a doctor had prescribed the chewing gum, worried that she'd chew through her fingernails or something else. Beaver was normally a bundle of nervous energy, but usually she was upbeat. Worrying about what had happened to Jeremy and everybody else, the wind had gone from her sails and she just looked anxious.

"They'll be okay," Erin comforted, reassuring Beaver with what she herself wasn't sure of. "Everything will turn out okay. Terry is seeing if he can find another way in, and the town is sending all kinds of volunteers and equipment. I've seen the way they work together. They'll find Jeremy and the others and get them out."

## APPLE-ACHIAN TREASURE

Beaver rubbed her face with her fingertips and shook her head. "Who else? Who is there with him?"

"Vic and Willie."

Beaver nodded. "Willie is good. He knows a lot about what to do in an emergency."

Erin agreed.

Someone else came through the woods toward them. Erin stared at the figure, trying to think of who it might be. As he got closer, she saw that it was a young man, an older teenager or man in his early twenties, slender, not yet filled in after his final growth spurt. His face looked familiar, but she couldn't think of who he was.

"What's going on?" he asked.

Erin frowned at him and opened her mouth to ask him his name. She figured he must belong to one of the nearby farms and had seen the unexpected vehicles or heard on the radio that something was wrong.

"Erin, do you know Cam?" Beaver asked.

Erin stared at Cam, her mouth open.

"Campbell Cox," the boy said. "You're Erin, right? You know my mom."

Erin nodded. "Mary Lou, yes," she agreed breathlessly. She looked at Beaver. "What's he doing here? You said that you knew him... I wondered..."

"We can't get into that," Beaver said. "But he can be trusted."

Erin looked at Cam for a minute, then nodded slowly. "Okay... but trusted to do what? What are you guys up to?"

Beaver looked at Erin for a minute. She shook her head and looked back at Cam. "There's been... an accident. A cave-in." She gestured at the mine.

Cam's face showed surprise. He looked around, as if expecting to see someone sneaking around, eavesdropping on their conversation. "That's not good. Do you think...?"

Beaver shrugged. "I don't know anything yet. But if this was intentional..."

Erin looked at the two of them, frowning so heavily that her head hurt. "What? What are you talking about? If this was *intentional?* It was a cave-in."

"We'll have to wait for the results of the investigation before we know that," Beaver said, shrugging.

"The results of what investigation?"

"Into the cave-in," Beaver said evenly.

Erin stared at her, shaking her head. "You think that somebody did this to them? Somebody caused this cave-in on purpose?"

"We don't know anything about it at this point," Beaver said. "All we know is what you have told us. That Vic and Willie and Jeremy went into the mine and then the cave-in happened. We don't know any more than that, and we only know that because you told us."

"Then what are you doing here?" Erin asked. "I thought you were here because you had heard over the police radio, so you came to help."

Beaver shook her head. "We've been… investigating other things."

"And that investigation led you here. To Orson Cadaver's farm."

"It's an interesting coincidence that this is where your mystery led you," Beaver contributed. There was a twinkle in her eye despite her worry for Jeremy.

Erin tried to understand what the connection between Beaver's investigation and her treasure-hunting could be, and couldn't come up with anything. Obviously, it had been a surprise to Beaver as well. She hadn't expected to find Erin and her friends there.

"What are we going to do?" Cam asked Beaver, looking toward the mine. "Can we call someone to help? And what about the town?" He gestured to the radio and addressed Erin. "Did you call the police? There's a volunteer fire department, they could help."

## APPLE-ACHIAN TREASURE

"Everyone is on their way," Erin told him. "Terry is already scouting around to see if there is an alternate way to get in."

Cam nodded. "Do you want me to take a look around?" he asked Beaver. "Make sure there isn't anyone else around?"

Beaver shook her head. "No. You'd better stay here with Erin. Make sure she's safe until Officer Piper gets back. I'll look around."

Erin expected him to argue. What young man wouldn't argue with a woman who told him that he needed to stay and take the safer course while she walked into danger? Every boy she had grown up with would have been offended by such a suggestion and would not have agreed without significant coercion. But Cam surprised her by not objecting. He just sat down beside Erin while Beaver got to her feet.

"Who are you looking for?" Erin asked. "I haven't seen anyone else around here."

Beaver chewed her gum and gave a loose shrug. "Just anyone who shouldn't be here."

"But everyone has been called to help, so pretty soon, everyone is going to be here, and you won't be able to tell…"

Beaver nodded with grudging respect. "You're right," she agreed. "So, I need to look around before everyone shows up. If there's anyone else hanging around this farm, I need to find them."

"I didn't see any other cars on the road on the way out here, and we parked by ourselves."

"They would at least think to hide their vehicle, I would think. That was one reason I was so surprised to see Willie's truck there, right out in the open."

Erin couldn't help the smile that started to creep across her face. "Did you think that Willie was involved? Everybody is always thinking that he's involved in criminal operations, but he's not. He got out of that, and he doesn't help the Dysons out any longer."

"Never trust appearances," Beaver said. "I have to assume that people are lying. I have to assume that when they say they're not involved, they really are, and I have to act as if it were true. As that old TV series used to say: 'trust no one.'"

"Willie isn't involved in anything. He's in the mine. He's one of the victims here. He's not involved in anything shady."

"Willie went in there with your friends," Beaver said slowly. "But that doesn't mean he was innocent. He may have been stabbed in the back by one of his cohorts. He might be working both sides. He might have taken Vic and Jeremy in there, fully intending to get them out of the picture."

Erin was shocked at the suggestions. It wasn't like she hadn't suspected Willie of shady dealings in the past. She had suspected him more than once, but he always came out innocent, and she didn't think he would ever get caught, even if he were involved in something. But to suggest that he had gone into the mine to rid himself of his girlfriend and her brother... there was no way. Erin knew that he loved Vic and there was no way he would ever betray her.

Beaver was studying Erin's reaction carefully. She nodded slowly to herself as she prepared to look for whatever conspirator she thought might be lurking nearby. "I hope not too," she said. "But I can't afford to trust anyone."

"Doesn't that include me, then?" Erin asked. Beaver had confided in her. She was leaving Erin there where she could cause more mischief. If anyone was to be suspected of causing the cave-in, Erin had to be the chief suspect. She had brought them there. She had allowed them to go into the mines while claiming that she herself was too scared to go inside. She was the one who could most easily have arranged for an accident to occur, all while she sat coolly outside and waited for help that she knew would arrive too late.

Beaver looked at Erin, then looked at Cam. "Keep an eye on her."

Cam nodded, understanding. Beaver walked away, and Erin turned her attention to the young man.

"I didn't do anything."

"I don't think you did," Cam agreed. "But we have to be careful. Beaver is really good at what she does. She wouldn't still be alive if she wasn't."

"What do you know about her? And what exactly are you doing with her? I don't understand how you're involved in any of this. You're an informant? Is that it? But why would she bring you here? I don't understand what someone as young as you could be doing that the federal agencies would be involved. I don't understand what you could do to help them."

Any answer that Cam might have had for Erin was swallowed up when the rescue teams from Bald Eagle Falls began to arrive. They came in groups that Erin assumed must have carpooled together, half a dozen helpers to a vehicle. Some carried rescue or aid supplies with them, food, or equipment Erin was unsure of. They were a strange combination of laughter and grim determination. Excitement to be part of a big disaster and rescue operation, and anxiety about how it was all going to turn out and if they were going to be able to save their friends from injury or death.

They greeted Erin and coordinated with each other, setting up equipment in the glade, going into the mine to have a look at the problem, and discussing the situation vigorously with each other. Erin wasn't sure who was in charge, but someone needed to coordinate everybody before they all started approaching the problem separately and ended up tripping over one another.

Terry returned from his scouting mission and tried to make himself heard above the babble of all of the volunteers.

"Can I get your attention, please? I need everybody to listen so that we can approach this in a coordinated effort and do everything we can to help Vic, Willie, and Jeremy."

The scattered volunteers quieted, listening to Terry's instructions.

"I want you to get together with your teams. Firefighters in a group, Scouts in another. People in charge of food. Communications. Get together with your group and make sure that you have a spokesperson appointed. We are going to manage all communication through that spokesperson so that I don't have to yell over all of this chaos."

People nodded and smiled their agreement.

"If you don't have a group, stand over here," Terry pointed. "We'll put you where you can be best used. Okay? It's going to be a while before any of the responders can make it from the city out here. I could use a few flagmen for traffic control, to help direct the city folk to the right route and make sure we're sticking to the established roads rather than just driving across private land."

A few hands went up. Terry looked around at them, nodding. "Don, maybe you could take charge of the flagmen and coordinate them."

The man he spoke to nodded agreement, and Erin watched them gravitate toward each other and start to make arrangements for who would stand where and what jobs they would have.

"I want to break this rescue into two approaches," Terry advised. "Until we have experts in here who can tell us otherwise, I want to go in two ways. First, clearing the rocks and rubble out of this entrance," he pointed to the mine entrance that Erin was already intimately familiar with. "There isn't a lot of room to work, but if we could run a line of people outside, passing rock from one person to the next like a bucket brigade, I think that's the quickest way to get rock out of the tunnel rather than just shifting it from one place to another inside. I don't know how much rock is in there… It's a lot. It might be a hopeless venture. But I need a team to get started."

There were nods of agreement.

"Secondly, I want to go in through another tunnel. K9 and I have been exploring some of the other mines and entrances, and I think we have one that has the potential of getting close to this tunnel here, after the cave-in. Assuming that the whole tunnel has not collapsed and that we still have a chance of getting to any survivors… I want to get together a team that can come up with a plan to dig or drill from one tunnel to the other."

He looked around at the grim faces. Everyone was now listening to him, no one was joking around.

"Get your groups together and appoint a spokesperson. I want to talk to the spokesmen in ten minutes." Terry looked at his watch and nodded, marking the time.

## Chapter Twenty-Six

ERIN WATCHED THE TOWNSPEOPLE organizing themselves and thought that she should attach herself to one of the teams, but she didn't have the energy to do anything but sit beside the radio listening for the updates on when the actual Search and Rescue team would be arriving from the city.

Erin saw a group of the church ladies setting up a folding table. There would be drinks and sandwiches for the volunteers. Erin would normally be there, coordinating the sandwich-making, setup, and distribution with Vic at her side. She looked at the radio, waiting for confirmation that trained rescuers were on their way.

Erin saw Mary Lou coming toward her, a confused expression on her face. Campbell scrambled to his feet.

"Mom!"

"Campbell. What are you doing here?"

"I… er… I was helping out Beaver."

"Beaver? Helping her with what?"

Campbell gave her a hug. "How are you, Mom? And Josh?"

"Fine. We're good. You don't answer my calls. I never know what you're up to."

"Sorry. Just getting myself settled. I get wrapped up and forget to call back until it's late, and then I don't want to call and wake you up."

## APPLE-ACHIAN TREASURE

Mary Lou brushed Campbell's cheek with a kiss, then held him at arm's length to look at him. Erin evaluated him silently as Mary Lou did. He appeared to be healthy. His color and weight were good. He didn't look like someone who was using drugs or partying every night. Erin would have guessed that he had a good job and a safe place to live. Mary Lou dropped her hands, nodding.

"You call me back anyway," she told him. "Even if it's late at night. I want to hear from you. Go ahead and wake me up."

He shrugged.

"I need to help out here... why don't you come tell me what you've been up to." Mary Lou gestured back toward the table where the ladies were setting up the refreshments.

Campbell's eyes flitted to Erin.

"I'm not going anywhere," she told him. "I want to be close to the radio."

He nodded and walked with his mother over to the table.

Beaver sat down close to Erin. She looked around, watching all of the volunteers hard at work. Her eyes lingered on Cam, talking to Mary Lou and helping her out at the refreshment table.

"So... what can you tell me about this Orson Cadaver? He was a distant relative of yours?"

Erin nodded. "Lots of years back. I don't know what I can tell you that you don't already know. He came into a lot of money, but nobody knew where it came from. Or no one told, anyway. It seemed like it could match up with the poem, but I don't know. It was only a guess." She stared at the mine entrance. "A guess I wish I hadn't made."

"It's not your fault. You couldn't have predicted that something was going to happen to Vic and the others. You wouldn't have let them go in if you'd thought that they were going to get hurt."

"I was worried... I did tell them not to go at the last minute... but by that time they were already all excited about going. I couldn't stop them."

"Did you have a premonition something was wrong?" Beaver asked. "Why did you tell them not to?"

"I was just... worried about them being underground, I guess. I'm... claustrophobic after what happened to me in the caves... I couldn't go down there if someone held a gun to my head." She considered for a moment. "Well, maybe if someone put a gun to my head. I did go in there to see what had happened. But I couldn't ever have gone down there to explore with them."

"So, there wasn't something specific that you thought was going to happen? Or anything that triggered the thought?"

Erin thought about it and shook her head. "No, I don't think so. Why?"

"I just wonder whether your unconscious mind had processed something that you weren't aware of consciously. There might have been something that tipped you off to someone else's presence here. Or that made you feel like they were in danger from someone specific."

"Whoever stole the first copies of those maps hit me over the head. They could have killed me. It obviously wasn't someone who had any qualms about using violence. If they're racing us to find the treasure... then that puts all of us in danger."

"Maybe," Beaver agreed. "So what about the cabin? You and Vic explored it?"

"Yes, but there really wasn't anything there. It's been over a hundred years since he hid the treasure... I guess I shouldn't have been surprised that we didn't find anything else. What kind of clue would have survived that long?"

"You never know. Sometimes the darnedest things survive... things you never would have expected to."

## APPLE-ACHIAN TREASURE

Erin sighed. "Well, not in this case. It seems like all that survived was the poem. And if it hadn't talked about moles, we never would have considered looking in the mines. Or maybe we would have, I don't know. But I wish we hadn't. I wish I'd never found that poem."

"But you did." Beaver's burning eyes betrayed her interest in hearing more about the treasure, maybe in finding it herself. "I know you don't have the poem anymore, but could you tell me again what it said? Do you have it written down anywhere?"

"Beaver..." Erin's voice broke and she cleared her throat to try to speak clearly. "They're trying to figure out how to get our friends out of a collapsed mine. If they're still alive. And you're looking for the treasure?"

"I've done everything I could to help. I'm standing by if there's anything else I can do. But in the meantime... why not look into the treasure? If the treasure is what is motivating someone to commit violence, even risking killing three innocent people in one blow, then we need to catch him. Don't you think?"

"Yes."

"Well, the only way we're going to catch him is if we know as much as or more than he does about the treasure. We need to get out ahead of him. We need to try to find the treasure before he does, if it still exists."

"You and Cam... is this about the treasure hunt, or about illegal drugs? I don't understand what it is you have to do with him?"

"Cam's a good boy. He's got a good heart. But he's going to end up in trouble if someone doesn't get him back on track. I hate to see anyone throwing their life away. I really do."

Erin nodded. "I know... I saw it in foster care... it only takes a few steps to go from being an honest, hardworking citizen to someone operating on the wrong side of the law, as if you had no conscience in the first place. I'd hate to see that happen to Mary Lou's son. I wouldn't want to see her hurt." Erin's eyes were attracted back to the entrance of the mine by a group of people who suddenly started talking louder, but then they quieted again and whispered among themselves, giving nothing away. "But I don't want my friends to get hurt either. He came here with you, right?"

Beaver took her time answering, chewing slowly on her gum while she watched Campbell with his mother.

"We came separately," she said finally. "We didn't want to attract attention by being seen together. We expected it to be deserted, no witnesses. When we saw the vehicles, I had to investigate further."

"So if you came separately, you don't know what he might have done before you got here."

"No. I don't."

"And he doesn't know what you did before he got here."

"No."

"And you both hid your cars, so no one knows how long you were here ahead of time and whether you were here before me and the others. Or whether you had time to rig up some kind of booby trap."

Beaver gazed steadily at Erin. "That's right," she agreed. "You know I'm a federal agent. What are the chances that I would give up my whole career to pursue some treasure that probably doesn't even exist?"

"You do hunt treasure."

"Yes, but I do it on my own time and I don't let it interfere with my job. And I don't mug women and collapse mines. That's an ethical violation." She gave a wide grin to signal that she was joking.

"But I don't know that. You could have been involved. I have no way of knowing."

"No, you don't," Beaver agreed.

"Then… I don't think I'm going to tell you anything else. You don't need to know the poem or anything else that we found out. You're on some other case and you just think it may link up to ours. You thought that maybe the two are linked somehow, but you don't know."

"Absolutely right," Beaver agreed.

Erin had expected at least some kind of argument from her. Why didn't she argue and say that she hadn't done anything? At least then, Erin would be able to examine whether what she said was true or not. She was thrown off kilter by Beaver's agreement that all of her conclusions were correct.

"You don't care?"

"Of course I care. But I also don't want you getting hurt or killed. It's better if you don't go around blabbing about the treasure. It's better if everybody just thinks that you have given up. That in the face of this disaster, it just doesn't matter to you anymore."

"And it doesn't," Erin agreed. "I really don't care how much money the gold is worth. It's not worth as much as my friends' lives."

Beaver nodded. She pulled a pack of gum out of her pocket and popped a couple of new pieces of gum into her mouth. She offered the package to Erin, who declined.

"What would you do if you came into a lot of money?" she asked conversationally.

Erin had determined that she wasn't going to answer any more questions, but this wasn't a question about the poem or the treasure. It was just a philosophical question.

"Uh... Well, I don't know. I'd pay Charley out on the bakery, if she'd let me. How much do you think the treasure would be?"

"It sounds significant from the description. Gold is always good. Hundred-year-old gold is even better. And if there are artifacts... things other than gold coins... then that's worth even more."

"Maybe."

"Of course. It all depends on what you find. Gold isn't always gold. It could be... oh, a family Bible, and Orson considered the word of God to be golden. Or it could be family relationships. Or a good crop. It could be something painted gold, or something considered valuable, or it could even be fool's gold, but he hoped it would lead him to a vein of real gold. There's no way for us to know what it was he really valued. At least, not based on the information you have so far."

Erin nodded. She had wondered a few times whether gold was really gold or not. It could mean anything valuable. Or it might just be a poem. There might not even be a treasure. Orson could have had his own fortune from somewhere else. Or he could have had nothing, and his wealth was just gossip run rampant. It was impossible to tell.

"Do you think there's anything hidden in the mine?"

"I think… if there was… It's probably either buried, or someone got here ahead of you. What are the chances that someone blew up the tunnel without knowing whether there was gold in it or not?"

"You think it was blown up?" A band of muscle tightened around Erin's chest. She had been thinking it, in the back of her mind. But she hadn't wanted to actually put it into words.

"Don't you?" Beaver asked.

"I don't know. I really don't. I don't want to think that anyone could be that… that wicked. Blowing it up intentionally when there are people inside… that's horrible."

"Is it more likely that it was an accident?" Beaver asked. "What are the chances of that?"

"We don't have any evidence that it was intentional. And I didn't see anyone around."

Beaver looked around at the woods. "There are plenty of places to hide. Even just going into another tunnel." She motioned toward the entrance to another mine. "You'd have to be pretty brave to take shelter in one tunnel while you cave in another. You'd have to be pretty confident that it wouldn't collapse the tunnel you were in as well. But I don't think it was an accident. These mines have been untouched for a hundred years. Willie wouldn't have gone inside if he hadn't thought it was safe. He's very experienced in the matter. You think he would make a mistake like that?"

Erin wiped her nose. "No."

"Me neither," Beaver agreed.

"So you think… someone got here ahead of us and set explosives to blow up when we went in?" Erin shook her head, having a hard time picturing it. "You think that they were watching to blow it up?"

"Who knows. Maybe they never intended to hurt anyone, and you guys were just in the wrong place when the charges had already been set. But I don't believe in coincidences."

"That's what Terry always says."

"Officer Piper is right. Sometimes there are coincidences, but more often, there really is a link, and not chance."

Erin covered her face, rubbing her eyes. She couldn't understand why she was so tired. She didn't want to do anything but lie down and go to sleep. Even though she knew her friends were trapped or buried in the mine, she couldn't think about it. Her brain didn't want to accept it. She just wanted to go to sleep and let everyone else deal with it. Maybe when she woke up, she'd be better able to deal with it.

"Let me get you a drink," Beaver offered. "Have you had anything?"

"No. I'm not hungry."

"You need to at least keep up your fluids. You don't realize how much you might be sweating off because you're just sitting around. It doesn't feel like you're doing any work, but your body still is." Beaver got up and went over to the table that Cam and Mary Lou were at. She said a few words to them, picking up water bottles and a couple of snacks from the table. She returned and handed one water bottle to Erin and held out a muffin and a granola bar. "Pick."

Erin picked the granola bar. She could eat it later when she really wanted it.

"How are they?" Erin asked, nodding to the Coxes.

"They seem to be handling it just fine," Beaver said with a shrug. "I don't think you need to worry."

"I do worry about my friends. And Mary Lou… she doesn't have very many friends left in this town. I want her to know that I still support her."

"I'm sure she knows that."

# Chapter Twenty-Seven

There was a sudden buzz of excitement. Erin looked around.

"What is it? What's going on?"

"Let me find out." Beaver got up and circulated with the volunteers, asking quick questions. She returned to Erin's side. "The Search and Rescue team is here. Lots of heavy equipment. Now we'll get something done."

"What? What are they going to do? They can't move the rock much faster than the volunteers have already been doing. You can only take out so much at one time."

"I'm not sure. But I'm sure we can put them to use."

Erin turned away from the gossiping volunteers who were straining for the first glimpse of the Search and Rescue team, and watched those who were still carrying rock out of the mine. There was a big pile that had already been removed. Some of the volunteers had no gloves and had bloody fingers. They all looked exhausted. They would continue to work until they dropped.

Terry hurried over from where he had been working in another mine and barely nodded at Erin. He jogged past her with K9 beside him, headed across the woods to where the vehicles were parked.

"Do you think they can do something?" Erin asked, following Terry with her eyes.

"He apparently has a plan."

They sat, waiting, their thoughts on those who were still trapped inside the mine.

There was a lot of equipment brought in, and Erin waited, wondering how long they would be stuck in the cave. What was the limiting factor? Air? Water? Injuries and shock? How long had it already taken and how much longer would it be before they could reach the tunnel? Was it already too late?

Erin held back tears, trying to keep herself under control as they moved the drilling equipment into the tunnel that Terry had picked out. There were engineers who walked around looking at the tunnel and the way that the walls were braced, how the rocks in the collapsed tunnel had fallen, and everything else that their eyes could see that Erin's couldn't. It seemed like it was going to take another two weeks before they would be able to decide whether the tunnel was stable enough for drilling. Erin didn't want to wait. Terry obviously didn't either, shifting back and forth from foot to foot while he waited for them to finish their inspection.

"If they say not to drill, what are you going to do?" Erin asked.

Terry's mouth formed a straight line. "They'd better not tell us not to drill."

"If they say it's not safe, are you going to chance it anyway?"

He shook his head slowly. Not in an answer of 'no,' but thinking it through and unable to make a decision. "I don't want to lose anyone else. I don't want to take the chance of another cave-in. I guess… we have to find a safe way in, or we look for something else. We can't take the chance of hurting someone else."

Erin had been afraid of that. If she were the one in charge, she would be more likely to tell them where they could stuff their engineering degrees and go ahead anyway.

# APPLE-ACHIAN TREASURE

Her friends were in there. The family she had chosen. She needed to get them out.

Finally, the engineers and the Search and Rescue team all huddled together in a little group with Terry and the other officers in the Police Department to discuss their findings and make a decision. Terry turned around and gave Erin a thumbs up. A cheer went up from the volunteers who were waiting for the decision just as intently as Erin was. Erin struggled not to cry. It was such a relief to know that they were doing something. No more sitting around waiting, moving rocks out of the way one at a time.

The drilling started.

Erin had no idea how far they had to drill or how long it would take. She held her breath at first, thinking that it would just be a minute or two and then Vic, Willie, and Jeremy would be free. But it went on and on.

Lights had been set up both inside the tunnels and outside where the volunteers were gathered, and they were needed as darkness fell. Erin nibbled on her granola bar. How could it take so long?

Her body was sore from sitting on the ground for so long. Every joint and muscle hurt. She got up and walked around a little, but that didn't do much to relieve the pain. Erin paced back and forth, willing them to finish the drilling and break into the next tunnel, as if she could make it go faster with the power of her mind.

There was a shout from someone, and the sound of the drill pulling away from the rock and then winding down. Erin and the others held their breaths. Was that it? Were they through?

There was a lot of talk, and eventually Terry came over to fill Erin in. "They're moving to hand tools now. If the maps are accurate, or at least close, then we should only be a few inches away from breaking through. But we don't want to injure anyone on the other side or take the chance of another cave-in if we cause instability in that wall. They'll drill a few small test holes, see if they can get any response from Vic and Willie and Jeremy and evaluate the best way to cut through the last little bit of rock."

"We're so close!" Erin clenched her fists, frustrated. "Can't we just drill the last bit?"

"We don't want to hurt them. We have to effect a safe rescue, not a fast one."

Erin growled and continued her pacing.

# Chapter Twenty-Eight

"THEY'RE ALIVE!"

Erin gasped with the rest of the volunteers. Then a cheer went up. Tears were racing down Erin's cheeks. She had never been so relieved in her life. She looked across the glade to Terry, a broad smile across his dust-smeared face. They were alive. She had been trying not to admit to herself that they might not be. They were experienced in cave exploration. They wouldn't have been caught in the collapsing tunnel. But she knew that there would have been no way for them to predict or avoid it.

Erin pushed her way through the volunteers to reach Terry, her legs quaking. Everyone else was trying to crowd closer as well, asking urgent questions, wanting more details. Terry tried to hold them off, using his strong cop's voice to make them back off and let Erin through. Eventually, she reached him.

"Tell me what you know! They're all alive? They're okay?"

Terry put his arm around her to pull her close, but spoke over her to the rest of the crowd. "They're all alive. They have injuries. We have paramedics standing by for when we get through the last few inches so that they can be treated and transported to the hospital right away. Now that we can communicate with them, we can be sure that they are far enough away from the wall for us to drill the rest of the way through. The engineers believe that we can get through the wall without destabilizing it, but we're still going to go slowly and make the smallest possible access hole to get them out. It will take few more minutes."

"Who's hurt? How badly?" people asked urgently.

"We won't know the full extent of their injuries until we get them out."

Erin looked at Terry, knowing that he was avoiding the question. If they were able to talk to the explorers, then they would have a pretty good idea of how badly they were hurt. Whether the injuries were serious or just minor. But he wasn't revealing anything to the public about how extensive those injuries might be.

Terry answered a few more questions. He gave Erin a squeeze and let her go. "It will be just a few more minutes," he promised. He returned to the tunnel.

The ambulances that had been waiting back where the rest of the vehicles were parked made their way slowly through the trees so that they would be right outside the entrance to the second tunnel as soon as everyone was brought out. Erin watched them get their equipment ready with a sick feeling in her stomach. Gurneys, IV bags, big cases of medical supplies. They kept their voices low and didn't answer any questions. Tom Banks and the sheriff kept the crowds back so that the paramedics wouldn't have to deal with them.

Then there was movement from the tunnel again. Not Terry returning to give them more news, but one of the Search and Rescue workers supporting Jeremy as he walked out. The young man was holding on to the worker, obviously weak, but he was walking under his own power.

A huge cheer went up from the crowd. Jeremy raised his head slightly to look at them, giving a vague nod. The Search and Rescue worker took him directly to the paramedics, who had him lie down on one of the gurneys and began to talk to him and ask him questions. Erin's attention was split between Jeremy and the entrance to the

## APPLE-ACHIAN TREASURE

tunnel, waiting for the next person. Eventually, it was Vic she saw, supported on either side. Upright, but not exactly walking under her own power as Jeremy had. Her face was white in the harsh lights.

They waited. It seemed like a very long time before they saw movement from the mine entrance again. Then two burly Search and Rescue workers struggled out, carrying Willie by the arms and ankles, stretched out between them.

A murmur went through the crowd, then another cheer. Everyone was out. They were all alive.

The crowd was surging forward, everyone wanting a better look at how the three friends were. They wanted to talk with them and get their stories. The Police Department and the Search and Rescue workers held everyone back, trying to keep a perimeter around the paramedics and the victims. Erin stayed where she was, watching every move of the paramedics, trying to figure out from their movements just how badly injured her friends were. They didn't move quickly, in a panic. But they were trained to stay calm and deliberate.

Willie appeared to be the most badly injured of the three, but the way the paramedics kept leaning over him, he was asking them questions and making demands regarding his treatment. The paramedics working over Vic and Jeremy touched them frequently to get their attention and ask them questions. All three had IVs in quick order.

Erin saw Tom letting Beaver past the perimeter to go to see Jeremy. Beaver looked back over the crowd and pointed at Erin, then motioned for her to come forward as well. Erin was encouraged by the volunteers and spectators to move forward.

"Go talk to them. See how they are," Mary Lou murmured to Erin as she helped to make space for Erin to get through. Erin's knees were shaking so badly, she didn't know if she could walk that far, but then in a minute she was there, looking back and forth between Willie and Vic, unsure which one to go to.

"Erin. Here. Come here." Willie had spotted her and was motioning impatiently for her to go see him. Erin obeyed, approaching the gurney and looking him over, a lump in her throat. He looked as he always did, grubby, skin darkened by his mining and processing work, but this time there was rock dust streaked with sweat and tears, his mouth a moist red slash across his face.

"Hey, Willie. How are you?"

"Busted my leg," Willie said tightly, motioning toward his right leg.

Erin ventured a glance toward it, worried that she would see white bone sticking out from a mess of bloody, broken skin, but Willie's pants had been cut away and an inflated air splint was in place. There luckily wasn't any obvious blood or gore.

Erin could only imagine how frustrated Willie would have been to be limited in his mobility when he wanted to be taking care of everyone else. He would not have liked relying on the others to move him around and not to be able to get up and assess the situation and try to get them out of there.

"They'll have you fixed up in no time," she reassured him. "They'll get a cast on that at the hospital and you'll be menacing everyone with your crutches for a few weeks."

Willie gave a grin that was more of a grimace. He caught her hand and pulled her closer. Erin leaned close to him, her face warming a little as the paramedics tried to work around her.

"That wasn't a natural cave-in," Willie told Erin. "You tell Terry. They need to look for signs of explosives."

Erin nodded. "They will. Beaver was already saying that she thought it was intentional."

"I think there was a booby trap. Something caught my foot. It was too late to stop. A tripwire."

## APPLE-ACHIAN TREASURE

Erin felt sick to her stomach. That meant somebody had not just wanted to blow up the tunnel to keep anyone else from discovering what they had found in the mine. They had wanted to kill or injure whoever came into the mine.

"I'm so sorry, Willie. I never thought… I never thought that something like this could happen. I knew somebody else was looking for the treasure, but I never imagined someone could do something like this."

"I know." He squeezed her hand. "This isn't your fault, Erin. It was deliberate."

She shook her head, trying to fathom it.

"How is Vic?" Willie asked.

"I don't know. I'll go over and see. She looked pretty pale."

"She was shocky. They need to treat her for shock, even if she doesn't have any other injuries."

"I'll go see her," Erin promised.

She pulled out of his grasp and moved over to the gurney Vic was being treated on.

"How is she doing?" she asked the paramedics.

They didn't stop their work to look at her. "Broken arm. No other major injuries apparent."

"Willie said to treat her for shock."

One of them looked up from the scrapes that he was cleaning. "Of course we are treating for shock. We're not totally inept."

"Sorry. Willie is worried about her. She's his girlfriend."

"We're taking care of her. Which would be easier if we didn't have any interference. She's ready to move, we're just waiting for word from triage as to how everyone is going to be transported."

Erin had seen a helicopter land close by. It couldn't land too near the mine because it was so heavily wooded, but it had found somewhere to put down a mile or two away. They would be able to get one of the three to the hospital much faster than the other two who followed along on the ground.

Erin looked at Vic's face. She hadn't responded to Erin's proximity, staring off into space as if she were deep in thought. "Are you okay, Vicky? You're going to be taken to the hospital soon."

Vic's eyes moved vaguely to Erin's face. "Erin? I'm gonna sleep for a bit longer."

Erin stroked Vic's silky blond hair. "Okay. You can sleep for a bit. I don't think you're going to be putting in a shift at the bakery in the morning."

In fact, Erin suspected that no one would be opening Auntie Clem's Bakery in the morning. Erin would be at the hospital all night herself, making sure that everyone was going to be okay. She moved out of the way of the paramedics to let them do their jobs. She looked toward Jeremy. Beaver was already there talking to him, and the paramedics probably didn't need yet another person trying to get information.

Beaver saw Erin's questioning look and left her spot at Jeremy's side.

"He's okay," she told Erin. "There are no obvious injuries, but I'm worried about any weak spots from his shooting, where he could be bleeding internally. The blast wave that he would have been exposed to if it was an explosion rather than just a rock slide…"

"Willie says it was explosives. He said he thought he tripped a wire."

Beaver swore and shook her head. "What kind of lowlife…" She stopped speaking to breathe and attempt to get her emotions under control. "I've dealt with plenty of treasure hunters before, and they can get very cutthroat about not allowing anyone else near what they consider to be clues or stopping them if they think they're getting close to finding *their* treasure. But booby trapping the mine with explosives… that's pretty bad, even for treasure hunters."

## APPLE-ACHIAN TREASURE

Erin nodded. She didn't know what Beaver might have run into with other treasures she had hunted for, but the idea of someone not even caring if they killed others was almost unbelievable. She wouldn't have thought it was possible.

"So, Jeremy's okay? He's talking?"

Beaver rolled her eyes. "He's talking, but that doesn't mean he's making sense. I guess he's still back there, trying to solve the clues."

"What's he saying?"

"He just keeps repeating lines from that poem. Forest gold. He says he didn't see it. He should have seen it." Beaver shrugged. "I don't think he's hallucinating. I think he's confused and not getting out what it is he wants to say. I want them to get him to the hospital as soon as possible."

"They're just deciding which one to airlift."

# Chapter Twenty-Nine

VIC WAS THE ONE they ended up airlifting to the hospital, with Jeremy and Willie following by ground in the ambulances. Erin was able to relax for the first time, knowing that they were out of danger and weren't going to die because she had decided to try to solve a puzzle. It seemed more than bizarre that her friends could be put in mortal peril just because of the words of a poem penned over a hundred years before. They didn't even know for sure that there was any gold. It sounded like the clues to a treasure hunt, but there was no guarantee that it was anything but a weird poem. Orson Cadaver might have written it, or it might have been someone else in his family, or even someone that Erin hadn't run across yet in her review of Clementine's genealogy files.

Most of the volunteers were on their way home. They had quickly broken down the tables, gathered up any trash, and gone on their way. They would have work and school in the morning. Erin's eyes lingered on one woman she couldn't place mingled with the familiar faces. She had seen her somewhere recently, but couldn't think of where.

"Are you okay, Erin?"

Erin looked around and saw Adele.

"I didn't know you were here. How long have you been around?"

"I've been here for a while," Adele said vaguely. "I've just been keeping to the background."

## APPLE-ACHIAN TREASURE

Erin knew that Adele was introverted, not someone who liked to spend a lot of time interacting with others, especially in crowds. It was a bit surprising that she would even be there, with all of the chaos and activity going on. Adele preferred the quiet of her woods and the company of Skye and her own thoughts.

Erin glanced up toward the sky to see if the crow was around, but couldn't see him. "Everything is being cleared up now," she stated the obvious. "You could go home."

But Adele wouldn't be heading to bed early. She would be doing whatever it was she did at nights when she wandered through the woods and lit candles and said her prayers or incantations.

"I know," Adele agreed. She looked around. "I thought, though, that I might say a blessing over this area. The evil that was performed here... you don't want it to taint the place. I thought it might be a good idea to leave it with a blessing."

"Oh." Erin nodded her head. If Adele wanted to perform spells, she would not want to do it while there were still women from Bald Eagle Falls around who might see her and decide that they didn't like having a witch around. "Yes, that sounds nice."

Adele smiled. "I know you don't believe in the efficacy of such things. But your friends were injured here, and we don't want that kind of bad feeling remaining in the place."

Erin shrugged. It didn't matter to her what rites Adele wanted to perform.

"Why are *you* still here?" Adele asked. "I thought you would be in the city at the hospital."

"I'm going to catch a ride with Terry once he's done."

"Oh, I see."

"I didn't bring my own car. I came with the others in Willie's truck. And that's evidence for now."

"Do you want me to take you?"

"No, he'll be finished before long. He wants to see how everyone is doing too. Poor Jeremy was still trying to figure out the poem, even though he was in shock. He just kept repeating the line about forest gold."

Adele looked startled. "Forest gold?"

"There lies there forest gold," Erin quoted. "I don't know where it is, if there is any gold, but maybe whoever got here ahead of us and booby-trapped the mine does."

Adele frowned, looking around. It was late and the woods were dark, other than where lights had been set up to mark the way. Adele turned in a large circle, staring down at the ground. Erin wasn't sure if she were already starting her blessing, or if Adele was doing something else.

"Here," Adele said, pointing down. "Do you remember this?"

Erin followed Adele's finger to a plant with yellow leaves and a small cluster of red berries. She was tired and it took a few minutes to remember.

"Ginseng," she looked at Adele for confirmation.

"Ginseng," Adele agreed. "Also known as forest gold."

Erin blinked. "Forest gold?" she repeated. "*This* is forest gold?"

"Wild ginseng is very valuable. Especially the older roots. Sangers made fortunes hunting wild ginseng and selling it to the Asian markets." Adele studied the plant. "This one looks very old. Probably no one has been harvesting over here for decades. They get grazed down by deer and rabbits, so you can't always tell the age from the number of leaves. If you dig it out, you can count the number of scars in the neck, and that will give you its age."

"But you can't make as much selling ginseng as you could back then, can you?" Erin asked. "You can buy ginseng at the store, it's cheap. They must cultivate it, so there wouldn't be much of a market anymore."

"There is still a market for wild ginseng. About one thousand dollars a pound, last I heard. Ask Jeremy."

## APPLE-ACHIAN TREASURE

"Jeremy? What would he know about wild ginseng roots?"

Adele cocked an eyebrow. "He works for Crosswood Farm, doesn't he?"

"Yes. That's where he was working. As a security guard."

"They grow simulated wild ginseng."

"What is simulated wild ginseng?"

"They do the best they can to simulate the wild environment. They don't plant it in fields or greenhouses, but in its natural environment, and then just keep animals and poachers away while it grows. That may be how these plants started out." Adele pointed to a couple other ginseng plants. "But they've been growing wild for a long time since then."

"So, Orson's fortune came from growing ginseng? That's what you think?"

"I haven't seen this many ginseng plants so close together before. Could the poem be about ginseng?"

Erin hesitated, thinking about it. She recited the poem slowly to Adele.

> The treasure it enfolds
> Where lies there forest gold
> A king's ransom hid amidst
> The warrens of the moles
> The gift of life to those who toil
> Each day to reap the sterile soil
> Be wise if thou would life preserve
> And no lord be forced to serve

Adele nodded slowly. "*Gift of life* and *life preserve* would fit, since ginseng is supposed to be sort of a cure-all. They grow in the ground, where the moles are. Forest gold. References to monetary value."

One thousand dollars a pound. Erin pictured a ten-pound bag of potatoes. That wasn't so much, and ten pounds of ginseng root would be ten thousand dollars.

"That's for five- or ten-year-old roots," Adele said, her eyes on Erin's face. "Some of these are much older. They've been known to go for huge sums at auction."

Around them, people were still cleaning up and hauling heavy equipment away. Terry was putting up warning signs and police tape around the entrances to the mines. All of them tramping through the unassuming little plants without a thought.

"Doesn't anybody know about this?"

"Not as many people know anymore, unless they work for a farm like Jeremy. Hopefully, anyone who came here today was too distracted to notice it. We should see if the Police Department will post guards overnight. Do you know who the land belongs to?"

"It's public land. We checked before we came to explore. Didn't want to get shot for trespassing. Orson might have held title for a while, but it was eventually abandoned. Too far from town, I guess."

"If you want to come back here to collect it, you're going to need a permit. Or get someone who has a permit. They take a while to be issued, and by the time you get back here, all of this could be gone."

It was hard to imagine walking away and leaving thousands of dollars in the ground. But it was also dark, and Erin was exhausted. No one would have the energy to start digging roots at that point, even if they did have the required permits.

"Would Jeremy have a permit?"

"I doubt it. He's not collecting plants, he's guarding them."

"A permit for what?" Erin was startled at Beaver's words. She hadn't seen or heard the woman approach.

"I didn't know you were still here."

## APPLE-ACHIAN TREASURE

Beaver gave a lazy shrug. "I'm still here. I'll head over to the hospital before long, but I wanted to make sure law enforcement here had everything they needed. Bald Eagle Falls is a pretty small place, and this was a big operation. That's a lot for one small police department to handle."

Erin nodded. "They did a really good job, though."

Beaver looked Adele over and raised an eyebrow. "Everything okay here? I'm surprised to see you here."

"I wanted to do my part," Adele said. "I may not enjoy mixing with large groups of people, but that doesn't mean I can't. I wouldn't want to leave my friends in the lurch. I needed to do something for them, however uncomfortable it might be."

She looked at Erin. She hadn't said anything about blessing the ground or whatever it was she planned to do once she had a bit of privacy. Beaver cocked her head to the side and looked at the two of them. She pressed her lips together and raised her hands slightly in a questioning gesture. "What's up? You look as nervous as a cat."

Erin supposed that was probably true. She was anxious and trying not to show it. She wasn't sure what to do with the sudden revelation from Adele. She looked at Adele, wondering whether she should say anything about the ginseng.

"Go ahead," Adele said. "We need to tell Officer Piper about it anyway."

Erin was still hesitant. Beaver was a treasure hunter. Erin wasn't sure how she would react to knowing that there was a treasure trove right under her feet. Beaver waited. Erin looked down at the ground, grimacing, trying to think of the best way to proceed.

"If you need to tell Terry, then go tell Terry," Beaver encouraged. "It sounds like it's out of my jurisdiction, whatever it is. You don't have to tell me anything."

Erin was again confused by Beaver's lack of ego. If she had been a federal agent on TV, she would have had a fit over Erin not answering her questions the instant they were asked. She would insist that Erin was required by law to answer her questions. She wouldn't cede authority to someone else, but would want to run the case herself, even if it were nothing to do with her department. But that was TV. Erin supposed she shouldn't expect real life to imitate television that closely.

"Yes… I guess I should tell him first. Then he can decide what needs to be shared. I don't want to share anything I shouldn't."

Beaver nodded her agreement. "Last I saw, he was over by the—" she turned and saw that Terry was still working around the entrances to the mines. "Well, you have eyes."

Erin nodded to Adele and walked over to Terry. He gave her a smile and a nod, stepping back to take a look at his handiwork.

"You're looking pretty tired. We'll be out of here before long. Do you want to go to the hospital or straight home to bed?"

"Before that… there's another problem."

Terry's shoulders sagged. He rolled his head as if working kinks out of his neck and took a deep breath. "Okay. What's our next problem?"

"Adele is here," Erin nodded in the witch's direction, "and she knows about plants and herbs and such…"

"Yes, of course she does. That's her thing."

"And it turns out that some of these plants…" Erin swept her hand around to indicate a number of ginseng plants among the underbrush, "are very valuable."

"Well, if she wants to harvest some of them, I don't see a problem. It's public land, and people have the right to gather medicinal plants on—"

"But not ginseng."

Terry blinked at her. "Ginseng."

## APPLE-ACHIAN TREASURE

"It takes a special license and Adele doesn't have one. And I don't just mean it's valuable as a medicine. I mean it's… worth a whole lot of money."

"How much money?" his voice was slightly irritated. He didn't want to be having a conversation about valuable plants when he had so much else to be done.

"A thousand dollars a pound for the roots. Maybe more, because some of these plants are so mature. It could be thousands of dollars for each root."

Terry's mouth dropped open. "Thousands of dollars? Are you serious?"

"Adele thinks that's what the poem was about. Ginseng is apparently called forest gold. People make their living off of collecting it in the wild, and these plants have been left to grow for a hundred years, some of them. If we don't leave someone on guard here, and those guys who blew up the mine figure out that the treasure is really ginseng rather than gold, next time we come out here it's all going to be gone and on the black market."

Terry scratched his rough-whiskered chin. "I see."

"It's illegal to harvest unless you have a license. Whoever is looking for the gold probably doesn't have a license, but that won't stop them."

"I see the problem." He looked around for a minute at the undergrowth, thinking it through. "I'll get Tom to stand guard tonight. Someone will need to take over in the morning. I'll have to find out what department is actually supposed to enforce these licenses, but I'm not sure they're going to be willing to send anyone to guard it indefinitely."

"Adele said that I can get a license. Then I can harvest some of it. I don't care about getting it all, but I don't want to see someone rushing in here and taking the whole crop without replanting it like they're supposed to."

"Alright. Let me get people onto this."

"I don't know if you should just leave Tom to guard it by himself. I wouldn't want him to get shot like Jeremy. He might not be as lucky. And it's so remote out here... no one would know if he was injured."

"Jeremy," Terry repeated, looking at her. "Jeremy was shot because of ginseng?"

"Apparently. I didn't know that's what he was guarding, but Adele is familiar with the farm he's been working on. She says they grow ginseng."

He shook his head. "I can't fathom people shooting each other over plants."

Erin couldn't help but smile. "You'd understand if it was marijuana or poppies, wouldn't you?"

He considered. "Those are more in my realm of experience."

"Or even just plain gold instead of forest gold. Until we found out that gold wasn't really gold, this made perfect sense, didn't it?"

"True." He nodded. "I'll get up to speed on this as fast as I can. In the meantime..." He nodded to Beaver. "Maybe you want to get a ride to the hospital with Beaver. I'm obviously going to be out here a little longer than expected."

"Okay. I'll see. Sorry about this..."

Terry nodded. He gave a smile, making the dimple in his cheek appear. "I'd rather know now than have something happen. At least this time, you're not in the middle of the action."

"Well... I almost was."

"I'll see you later. Or tomorrow."

Erin went back over to Beaver and Adele, who didn't appear to be hitting it off. Erin found both women easy to get along with, so she wasn't sure why they treated each other with such wariness. But Adele was hard to know, and if she didn't want to share her reason for being there with Beaver, then that, together with the fact of who her husband was, would be enough to raise Beaver's suspicions about her motives.

"Beaver, are you going to the hospital soon?"

# APPLE-ACHIAN TREASURE

"That's the plan. Officer Piper doesn't want me to stay around?"

"No. He suggested I ask you for a ride to the hospital."

"Sure, of course. Are you done here?"

Erin nodded. There wasn't any reason for her to stay around. Adele wanted to be left alone to deal with her blessing and Terry needed to make sure that the land was properly guarded before he could leave. Erin wanted to get to the hospital and get an update on how her friends were all doing.

"Let's hit the road, then," Beaver agreed. She motioned for Erin to go with her and pulled out a flashlight. "Follow me."

She struck off across the glade. Erin shook her head. "The road is out this way."

"If you go for parking on roads where anyone can see you," Beaver agreed, and gave a grin. "Some of us don't like to paint targets on ourselves."

"Oh." Erin followed Beaver. They worked their way around the house and the debris where other buildings had been built. Erin stopped, looking toward the house. She couldn't really see it; she could just sense that the darkness was a little blacker and more solid there. "We should probably check out the house before we leave."

Beaver looked toward it. "You looked at it earlier, didn't you? You didn't find anything there. I didn't find anything there. There wasn't anyone hanging around the house, everyone stayed toward the mines, where you would expect."

Erin thought about the little house, and about the root cellar beneath it. "I think… maybe I should go in. There's something I should look at."

Beaver raised the flashlight toward Erin's face and paused, looking at her.

"Okay," she agreed. "We'll go check out the cabin."

She and Erin picked their way toward the house. It seemed like it was a lot farther away than it should be, having to watch every step to get there. Eventually, Beaver shone the light on the building. "There it is. You want to go in?"

"Yeah."

Beaver didn't head for the door. "You want me to go in?" she asked finally, as if reluctant to do so.

"It's not haunted."

"Maybe it is, maybe it isn't. I'm not in the habit of going into abandoned buildings late at night."

"We both looked at it before. There's nothing there." Erin took a couple of steps toward the door, trying to convince herself as much as she was trying to convince Beaver.

"Then why do we need to look at it again?"

Erin kept moving toward the cabin. She put her hand on the door handle and it turned in her hand. "It will just take a minute."

Beaver walked her in and shone the flashlight around at the walls. It was very dark. It was just as bare as it had been when Erin had visited it earlier. Erin pointed toward the trap door.

"There's a cellar."

"You want to go down to the cellar?"

"I don't *want* to."

"Then how about we leave it? It's been empty for a hundred years. We don't need to."

"I need to look at it again."

Beaver shrugged and moved toward it. She raised the trapdoor and shone the flashlight down the black hole. "Nothing there."

"Hold the light on me so I can see."

The other woman didn't object. Erin could hear her chewing on her gum. Erin did *not* want to go down that hole. It didn't matter that she had gone down before and hadn't found anything. It didn't matter that she had seen it already.

# APPLE-ACHIAN TREASURE

She just didn't want to go down there. It was a dark hole in the ground and no one would want to go down there.

It was difficult to find her footing and she went down the steep stairs unsteadily, constantly worried that she was going to fall down and break her leg. She had a flashback of the splint around Willie's leg. She did not want one around hers.

There were no more steps. Her feet were flat on the floor.

"Can you see anything?" Beaver asked.

"No. Do you want to pass me the flashlight?"

"Not particularly, no." Erin could see it flickering over her head as Beaver shone it around.

Erin pulled out her phone and turned it on. Her power was getting low, but she had enough for a few minutes. She used the screen rather than the flashlight LED to take a quick look around the room. The box in the corner was still there. She went over and looked at the lumps of dried-out roots in the bottom. Potatoes? No. Ginseng. That was what Orson had been harvesting. That was his treasure. Erin used her shirt as a basket and piled the remains of the hundred-and-fifty-year-old ginseng into it. Then she awkwardly climbed back up the ladder.

Beaver looked at the dirty collection of roots. "This is what you came looking for?"

"This is gold," Erin said.

"This?"

Erin nodded.

# Chapter Thirty

BEAVER GOT JEREMY'S INFORMATION from the reception desk and headed to his room, while Erin got Vic's and Willie's and tried Vic's room first. She wasn't at all surprised to find Willie sitting in a wheelchair beside Vic's bed instead of in his own room. His leg was in a cast, but other than that he didn't look any the worse for wear for his experience. The staining of his skin meant she wouldn't be able to tell if he was pale or if he had bags under his eyes anyway, but he looked bright-eyed and alert.

"Didn't they give you anything for the pain?" Erin asked. "I thought you'd be knocked out." She motioned to Vic, who was sleeping peacefully, her arm in a cast resting on top of the bed sheet.

"I didn't want anything," Willie admitted. "They insisted they couldn't set it without giving me something, but they kept the dose low, so I'm doing pretty well."

"But you must be in a lot of pain. Wouldn't it be better to sleep?"

He shook his head. "I want to hear what you found out."

Erin opened her mouth to protest that she didn't know anything. Then she stopped. Willie leaned forward.

"You always know something, Erin. I want to know what you figured out."

"It was Adele, not me."

"But you know, so spill. They booby-trapped the mine, didn't they?"

This Erin already knew from what she'd overheard from Terry and the other officers. She nodded. "You were right about there being a tripwire. They're going to have an expert come and look at everything, but Terry said he doesn't think it was an expert. Maybe someone who has used explosives for small jobs like stump removal. They only put the charge in one place, instead of in series along the tunnel."

"That's what saved us. If they'd strung it out ahead and behind us…"

Erin closed her eyes, not wanting to think of the devastation that would have caused. "Maybe it was only meant as a warning. Maybe it was only supposed to scare us off."

Willie nodded. "Yeah, it's possible. They cut off our exit, but assumed we'd be able to get out another way. The map wasn't very clear. I figured when I looked at it that we had multiple ways out. Maybe there used to be, or maybe the map was drawn to illustrate what he wanted to have done, not what had already been done."

Erin looked at Vic. "So how is Vic?"

"She's fine. They just wanted to keep her under observation, because of shock, but I'm sure they'll let her go tomorrow. I haven't heard how Jeremy is doing, but hopefully we can all go home tomorrow."

Erin nodded and blew out a breath. "I was so worried. I didn't know what kind of shape you were going to be in when we got to you. If we could get to you."

"The town really came together. There have been people trickling in and out of here all night."

"Yeah. It's really something to see. Bald Eagle Falls really knows what to do in an emergency."

Willie reached over to the bedside table and sipped a cup of water with a straw. "What else?"

"What?"

"You know something else. What is it?"

"Well... we found it."

"Found what?" Willie's eyes widened. "The gold?"

Erin nodded. She proceeded to tell him about the wild ginseng. Willie sat back, thinking about that.

"My grandmother used to gather sang. I never heard her call it forest gold."

"I guess it's really valuable. It's endangered now. You have to have a license to harvest it."

"Orson Cadaver was selling sang."

"That's what it looks like."

"Who would have guessed."

A nurse poked her head in the door. She looked at them and focused her attention on Willie. "You, sir, are not supposed to be here. Do you know how many people are looking for you?"

Willie grinned. "I'm where I'm supposed to be."

"You are supposed to be in your bed sleeping. Now off you go."

"I can't stay here with my girlfriend?"

"No."

"I'm not going to sleep in my bed. At least here, I can rest if I know she's okay."

The nurse strode into the room. Willie released the brakes on the wheelchair. "Okay. I'm going."

She stood with her hands on her hips, watching him go. She didn't assume he was really going to do what he was told. When he was gone, the nurse turned to Vic and checked her vitals.

"You seem to be spending a lot of time here," she said to Erin.

"What?" Erin studied her. She had seen the woman before but couldn't remember where from. The nurse's name tag said Chantel.

"You were here not so long ago after being mugged."

## APPLE-ACHIAN TREASURE

"Oh, yes I was," Erin admitted. "I'm sorry, I don't remember you."

"A knock on the head will do that to you. You're looking a lot better."

"I'm fine now." Erin put her hand over the bump on the back of her head. It was tender, but she didn't feel like she had after being hit. The pain, nausea, and shakiness had subsided quickly, and though it wasn't fully healed, she hadn't thought much about it.

"You should be more careful, wandering around out there in the dark," the nurse said. "Something could happen to you. This time, it was just a knock on the head, who knows what it might be next time."

"I know," Erin agreed. She'd been through enough dangerous situations to realize that things could always be worse. The head injury she'd sustained after first moving to Bald Eagle Falls had been much worse and she'd been afraid she wasn't going to make it. She shook off the images. "But I wasn't out there wandering in the dark. I was going to my car. I even had a security guard walk me out. I wasn't taking chances."

"Still, you don't want to go around taking unnecessary risks. Maybe you should listen to your boyfriend and take up another hobby."

Erin frowned. That wasn't part of the conversation she'd just had with Willie, but one she'd had with Terry when Jeremy had been in the hospital.

"Do I know you?" she asked. "I'm sorry, but are you from Bald Eagle Falls? Or do I know you from somewhere else?"

"No. Just someone you have had the serendipity of crossing paths with." The nurse fiddled with her watch. "Your friend here is going to be just fine. But if the two of you want to keep it that way, I would think about what people are saying. Just mind your bakery and leave the sleuthing to people who are properly trained."

"Umm… okay." Erin nodded. It wasn't like she hadn't heard that advice before. Obviously, Nurse Chantel had overheard one such conversation. "Thank you for your advice."

The nurse looked at her for a moment, as if expecting something more, then she nodded briskly and left the room.

# Chapter Thirty-One

ERRY WAS TIRED, BUT he was off duty and Erin was sure he'd go home and crash for a few hours very soon.

"You and Adele were right about the ginseng, of course," he advised. "We've called the Department of Environment and Conservation, and they are trying to coordinate someone to keep an eye on the farm; but they don't have their own security force, so they're having to scramble to figure out what they can do. In the meantime, we don't have a large enough team to take over security there as well as maintain order in Bald Eagle Falls, so they are looking at using some other department's agents to keep an eye on things for a while. Who knows, maybe Beaver will end up being one of the people out there guarding it."

"That would be funny. Although I'd be a little worried about her making off with some of the ginseng…"

"Why would you say that?"

Erin shrugged. "I just get the feeling that… she might not be the most… *honest* agent. That's not the word I want… but I'm always wondering what she's up to. She seems like she always has something else going on. Do you have any idea what it is she's been doing with Campbell?"

"Campbell?"

"Cox. Mary Lou's oldest."

"No, I'm not aware of anything. Why? What do you think she's been doing?"

"I don't know. Using him as a confidential informant, maybe. I can't think of anything she would have to do with a teenager like that."

"I guess CI is a possibility. Kids tend to be able to worm themselves into some unhealthy situations. But I don't think that means Beaver is doing anything she shouldn't be."

"You don't think she's the one who set the explosives in the mine, do you?"

Terry sat down and stared into Erin's eyes. "What?"

"It's just that… she was suddenly there. Not in an official capacity, but she was there before anyone else, other than you. And I think… she might have actually been there before you, and just hadn't made herself known to us. I think she and Campbell were already on Orson's farm for some reason."

"What reason could they have? You don't think she was there as a treasure hunter, do you?"

"Why not? You know that's her hobby. This thing with Campbell, I don't think it's official. I think she just knows him personally. She could have been there ahead of us, and she might have had a chance to search the mines and set the charge, booby-trapping it for when one of us came along to see it."

Terry shook his head and took a sip of his coffee. "You think she tried to blow up her own boyfriend?"

"I don't think she knew he was going to be there. She probably thought he was still too injured from being shot and would be staying at home, not out exploring caves with Vic and Willie. I don't think she meant to blow *him* up."

"But you think she set the explosives that injured them. That she didn't care about blowing up Willie and Vic."

Erin sighed. She ran her fingers through her hair. "I don't know. I don't know what to think. I just know… she was on the farm before anyone else. She implied that her case had led her there. But how would a case have led her to exactly the same place as we were going? The Orson farm had been deserted for a hundred years, untouched by anyone, and suddenly it's the center of a treasure hunt *and* a drug investigation? It doesn't make any sense."

"How would she have found out about the Orson farm? Did you tell her? You don't think she's the one who stole the maps at the hospital, do you?"

Erin considered. Could Beaver have hit her over the head and stolen the maps and her purse? Could she really have done that to someone she pretended was a friend? Erin's impression was that it had been a man, but with Beaver's boxy silhouette when wearing her hunting jacket, and her long, loping stride, she might easily be taken for a man at only a quick glimpse in the dark.

"We told her about the farm. Showed her pictures of it. I never thought… I mean, I knew she was a treasure hunter, but I didn't think she'd ever do anything to hurt anyone. I thought there was… some kind of code, that you wouldn't go after the treasure that your friend was looking for. Or that you would only do it together."

Terry nodded slowly. "I guess I'll have to look into it," he admitted. "I'm not sure who to talk to… I don't want to take any flak for throwing aspersions on a decorated agent."

"I know. I don't want to either. But I thought you would want to know. There was so much going on that day, I didn't know if you knew when she got there."

"You're right. It's the kind of thing I definitely want to know about."

When Erin went by Jeremy's room to see how he was doing, she expected to find Beaver there beside his bed, as she had found Willie sitting by Vic. But Jeremy was sleeping and there was no one else in the room. Erin moved around to the side of the bed and looked down at him, trying to assess his condition.

He had an IV line into his arm, but there were no machines monitoring his vital signs, no catheter bag as far as she could see, and no respirator or casts. He seemed like he could just be sleeping. Maybe the reason Beaver wasn't there was because Jeremy was fine, so she had gone home to sleep.

"You want something, or are you just going to stand there?"

Erin jumped and looked down at Jeremy, his eyes looking up at her, squinting against the brightness of the room.

"Sheesh, you scared the heck out of me. I thought you were asleep."

"Well, I was, but people keep coming in and looking at me."

"I'm sorry. I didn't mean to bother you. Just wanted to see how you are doing."

Jeremy lifted his hand to cover a yawn. His limbs seemed to be working perfectly normally. "How about Vic and Willie? Are they okay?"

Erin sat down in the chair next to the bed. "Yes, they're okay. Willie has been up and around. Well, as much as he can with a cast on his leg. Vic is sleeping, but she's not in any danger. And you're okay?"

"Needed a good nap, that's all. The doctors say there's nothing wrong with me. None the worse for wear for my adventure."

"Beaver said… when you came out, you kept saying that you should have seen it. The forest gold."

Jeremy dropped his eyes. He looked embarrassed. "It was right there in the poem, the whole time. I didn't know why I didn't catch on. I mean, you would think that with what I was doing… I would have seen it immediately."

"The ginseng."

He rolled his eyes. "In my defense, I don't spend all day at work staring at the plants. Mostly, I'm looking at the perimeter, watching for any movement. The plants themselves... they're just background. Something pretty to look at."

"But when you came out of the tunnel, you saw it."

"I figured it out just before that. I'd been in and out, and I guess my unconscious mind decided to unlock the puzzle for something to do. I realized that there was just as much ginseng in these woods as there was at work, maybe more. And it wasn't being guarded or claimed by anyone. Just like... gold in a mine."

"Do you think... that Beaver knew about it before you said anything? Or that Willie knew before he went in with you?"

Jeremy shook his head, frowning. "No. No one else knew."

"Somebody knew. Somebody was there ahead of us."

"We don't know that."

"You know it wasn't just a cave-in, right? It was caused by an explosion. Not just old explosives left behind, and not just something that was on a timer or remote detonated. It was a tripwire. They meant to catch whoever was there in a trap, maybe to kill them."

"Then asking whether Beaver knew is ridiculous. She wouldn't have rigged explosives up to blow me up."

"She didn't know you were going to be there."

"No, we didn't tell anyone ahead of time what we were doing, so she couldn't have known that."

"Then she could have set it up to trap Vic and me whenever we went back to look at the mine."

"Beaver wouldn't do that. She likes you guys."

"You've only known her for a little while."

"You don't think I would know whether she was a good person or not? The kind of person who would kill my sister?"

"She's trained in deception."

"It's not Beaver, Erin."

"Then what about Willie?"

"Why would he trip his own explosives? He could have been killed."

"But he's been mining for a long time. He probably knows how to handle explosives."

"He broke his leg! Rocks fell down all around us. The roof caved in. He broke his leg and could barely move."

"That part could have been an accident." But Erin didn't really believe that either Willie or Beaver had been involved, and Jeremy's reaction confirmed her instinct.

"There's no way Willie knew there was a tripwire down there. There's no way he would have led us in there and set off an explosion. No way."

"Okay. I just wanted to make sure."

A nurse bustled into the room. "I see our patient is awake. How are you feeling, Mr. Jackson?"

"Good," Jeremy approved. "Ready to go home."

"We'll have to talk to the doctor about that."

Erin looked at the time on her phone. She hadn't been in there for very long. Jeremy had been awake only a couple of minutes.

"How did you know he was awake?"

"I have eyes, don't I?"

"But you couldn't see whether or not Jeremy was awake. Not from out there."

She raised her eyebrows, then pointed to a small camera with a red light on it up in the corner of the room.

"Big Brother sees all."

Jeremy and Erin both looked at the camera.

"You have patients under surveillance?" Erin asked.

"We have to know if someone gets up and is wandering around or falls down and needs assistance. And the nursing staff is monitored to make sure they are providing proper patient care." The nurse rolled her eyes. "Washing our hands and not slapping the patients around."

Erin was aware of stories that had made it to the news of nurses being cruel to patients or ignoring their needs,

## APPLE-ACHIAN TREASURE

especially at nursing homes. "So you can see what's going on from your nursing station out there... all the time?"

"We sure can."

"What about patients' right to privacy?" Jeremy demanded. "Do you have cameras in the bathrooms too? This is outrageous!"

"I told you, it's for your own safety. Don't go getting all worked up. There aren't any in the bathroom. Just outside, with a timer so we know if someone has been in for too long."

Erin could hardly tear her eyes from the camera to look at the nurse. "Do you have sound too?"

The nurse hesitated before answering. "The sound is turned off unless we need to hear what's going on."

"So you *can* listen in whenever you want."

"Whenever it is *necessary*," the nurse asserted, "for patient safety."

Erin looked at Jeremy. He cocked his head slightly, eyebrows raised. Erin stood by while the nurse performed a brief examination in silence, her eyes darting nervously to Erin several times, then she hurried out of the room after a forced smile and "I'll update the doctor. We'll see if he's ready to discharge you."

Jeremy looked at Erin. "Well?"

"I think I know who made it to the mines ahead of us."

# Chapter Thirty-Two

CHARLEY HAD STOPPED BY to see Erin before taking a trip home to Moose river for the weekend.

"You're getting along okay with your mom?" Erin asked.

Charley wrinkled her nose. "I don't know. She won't stop trying to... mother me. It's like she has no clue that I'm an adult now and can make my own decisions. Every time we talk, she's trying to poke her nose into my life and make sure that I'm not getting into any trouble. Always telling me what I should do. She doesn't trust that I can make good decisions. It's aggravating."

Erin nodded. "But you're going back for a visit."

"Yeah. She is my mom, and I should make sure that I see them now and then. She's right about that, and so were you. I might feel smothered by her, but at least I've got a mom and dad around. I should enjoy that while I can."

"Exactly. I wish I still had my parents... though in all honesty, who knows what kind of a relationship we'd have. They weren't exactly a well-functioning unit. We all just have to take what we get and make the most of it."

Charley gave a shrug. "What is the matter with that rabbit?" she demanded.

Erin looked down at Marshmallow, who kept squirming and digging his way under the couch, and then dashing out and zig-zagging around the room. Orange Blossom, spooked by his wild behavior, was perched up on the back of the couch, watching him with ears back and eyes narrowed.

"I'm not sure. I was wondering if maybe he hit puberty, he's been so wild and crazy lately. But he's neutered, so Doc says it shouldn't be hormones. I think it might be the ginseng in the yard. I can't keep him out of it when I take him outside. He just makes a beeline straight for it."

"Well, if it makes a rabbit that frisky, I can see why the Chinese think it could be a magic elixir for humans."

Erin heard a truck engine outside and looked out the window to see Willy pulling up to the curb. Vic leaned over to kiss him goodbye, and then got out of the truck and headed to the house. She let herself in the front door and nodded to Charley.

"Saw your car was here and thought I'd stop in and say 'hi' before settling in for the night."

Charley looked at her watch. "I need to be getting out of here. I told my mom I'd be there before ten."

"You'd better get a move on, then," Vic agreed. She cocked her head at Erin. "And I wanted to check… no word on that nurse?"

Erin put her lists to the side and wrapped her arms around her knees. "No. I'll let you know once I hear, right now they won't say anything except that they're investigating. But I know she's the one who got to Orson's farm ahead of us. Only the person with the maps could have. And that was somebody at the hospital. She knew way too much about the conversations I'd had with Terry and Willie. She didn't just happen to overhear a few words. She had to be monitoring us."

"But she couldn't be the one who hit you, could she? And why would she set explosives to go off when we went into the mine?"

Erin twisted a lock of hair around her finger, frowning. "She must have had someone helping her, because I'm sure she wasn't the person following me at the hospital when the maps were stolen. And they must have figured that the explosion would look like just a collapse. If one could collapse, then anyone would consider it too dangerous to explore the rest of the mines for treasure, and they could do it at their own convenience."

"But we could have been killed."

"I know," Erin agreed. "And I don't think she cared if we were."

Erin had initially hoped that Terry would be able to arrest Nurse Chantel right away. Erin *knew* she had listened in on her conversations and plotted to find the treasure before Erin and to blow up the mine with people still in it.

But of course, the nurse was not in Officer Piper's jurisdiction and the police couldn't just rely on Erin's hunch, no matter how convincing. By the time they were ready to take any action everyone had been released from the hospital and was back in Bald Eagle Falls.

Erin and Vic were hard at work preparing for the Fall Fair when they finally got word that an arrest had been made.

Terry leaned up against the display case to fill them in on the details.

"The same surveillance system that allowed her to listen in on your conversations also proved what she was doing. We figured Nurse Chantel would be the one to break down and admit what she and her boyfriend had done when confronted with the truth. But it ended up being the boyfriend who confessed to the whole thing. It seems that Nurse Chantel wasn't one bit bothered that three people were injured in the explosion. In fact, she went to see each of them to see just how badly they'd fared." He shook his head. "The hospital had surveillance video of her checking in on each of them. You know how she was in checking on Vic while you were there?"

Erin nodded.

## APPLE-ACHIAN TREASURE

"She wasn't even assigned to that unit," Terry said. "She busted in there making it sound like she was in charge, but she wasn't. She just wanted to get a peek at her handiwork."

Erin shook her head. She glanced over at Vic. "Can you believe it? Someone in a profession like that, and she doesn't even care about people getting injured or maybe even killed."

"Maybe that's why she's a nurse," Vic contributed. "She might actually get a kick out of it."

Erin shuddered. "Unbelievable. I'm glad she didn't confess, because that means she won't get a deal, right?" She looked at Terry.

"Nope. The lowlife who knocked you out and set up the explosives might, but she won't."

"Good." Erin got a cookie out of the case for Terry. "Chocolate chip?"

"My favorite. I also hear through the grapevine that your ginseng harvesting permit has been approved. You should get the notice any time now. That means you'll be able to go out to Orson's farm to harvest, when you want. No more being on your feet all day to run Auntie Clem's. Dig a few more roots, and you can retire in style."

Vic looked at Erin, her mouth dropping open. "You're going to close Auntie Clem's Bakery?"

Erin shook her head, laughing. "Not a chance! I might hire a couple of other people so we don't have to put in such long hours, but I'm not quitting! I didn't work this hard just to retire to the easy life the first time I found a root worth thousands of dollars."

"They're not *all* going to bring in that much."

Erin knew they wouldn't all be worth as much as one of the old ginseng roots she had retrieved from Orson's cellar, which she had already put up for private auction, but with the number of plants that had been growing on the farm for decades, they could make a comfortable living, as long as it didn't become known where she was getting her money or where she was harvesting the ginseng.

"I have enough to buy Charley out," she said. "If she wants me to. Enough to hire new employees. And maybe if you want to travel, we could go on a vacation or two."

The morning of the Fall Fair was bright and clear. The air was crisp and the sun was shining brightly. Erin checked to see that everything was properly wrapped and arranged at her stand, but Vic had already taken care of everything, even with her arm in a cast.

"You don't have to do anything but smile and accept the compliments today," Vic said. "You did an amazing job on everything. All of your lists are checked off. Now it's time to enjoy yourself."

"I feel like I need to do something," Erin objected.

"Go look at all of the booths. And at the animals and other contest entries. There's lots to see."

"Okay, but I'll come to spell you in a while, so that you get a chance to look around too."

"And we shut down at three o'clock for the awarding of prizes."

Erin nodded. "I'm excited to see who wins. Did you notice that Mary Lou put a jar of jam in the preserves competition?"

"I did! So maybe Jam Lady Jams isn't dead after all."

Erin left Vic to man the booth and wandered among the other displays of quilts, preserves, and all kinds of arts and useful crafts. The variety was stunning.

"I hear you entered something in the baking competition."

Erin turned to see Adele. "Hey, I didn't expect to see you here. Yes, I do have an entry in the baking competition. But I can't tell you what it is."

"I'm patient. I'll find out when they award the prizes."

## APPLE-ACHIAN TREASURE

Erin felt herself blushing. "Well, maybe, but it's my first competition, so I'm not counting on winning anything."

Adele just smiled.

# Chapter Thirty-Three

ERIN COULDN'T HELP BUT be excited and nervous at the awards ceremony. The sheriff was announcing the winners and had been on the tasting committee.

"As always, the baking competition was a tight race. Everything was delicious. The judges tasted, consulted, loosened their belts, and tasted some more." The sheriff jiggled his heavy belt ruefully, drawing laughter from the crowd. "In first place, with a traditional Tennessee dessert, was the mile-high Apple-achian Stack Cake!" Sheriff Wilmot ripped open the envelope. "By Erin Price, of Auntie Clem's Bakery!"

Vic gave a whoop and did a little victory dance. Erin couldn't suppress the big grin that spread across her face.

"I suppose since this came from Auntie Clem's Bakery, that it is gluten-free?" Wilmot directed the question to Erin over the heads of the crowd.

Erin nodded and called back. "Yes, it is!"

"And the entry said that there was a special ingredient included to honor Tennessee's history," Sheriff Wilmot read from the card. "Are you going to reveal that ingredient?"

"Yes. I added ginseng."

"Ahh. There was a time when ginseng grew wild in these parts," Wilmot observed. "Now you have to go out of the county to find it, but maybe one day we'll have it growing wild again here."

Erin nodded and smiled. "Maybe so."

# APPLE-ACHIAN TREASURE

Erin spotted Mary Lou later in the afternoon as they were cleaning up their booth.

"How did you do?" Erin asked her.

"Not too badly," Mary Lou said, allowing herself a small smile and smoothed her well-fitted blazer jacket over her hips. "I got first in two categories."

"Not bad?" Erin repeated. "That's great!"

"The preserves don't get as many entries as the baking," Mary Lou said. "You did much better than I did coming in first in baking. The competition was much fiercer."

Erin shrugged self-consciously.

"And Beaver and Jeremy both placed in the target practice," Mary Lou told her. "Jeremy will have to live down the fact that his girlfriend beat him with a gun."

Erin laughed. "At least he has being shot and blown up recently as an excuse."

Mary Lou chuckled. "You must be excited about the prize. Who are you going to take?"

Erin frowned. "What?"

"On the cruise."

Erin shook her head, confused. "What cruise?"

"The first prize is an Alaskan cruise. Didn't you know that?"

"Oh! No, I didn't realize..." Erin had accepted the envelope from the sheriff, assuming it would be a gift certificate for dinner at the family restaurant or a small honorarium. An Alaskan cruise? "I guess... Vic... or Terry... oh boy." How was she going to decide between taking her best friend and her boyfriend? She would be more comfortable with taking Vic, uncertain whether she and Terry were ready for some big romantic trip, but choosing her closest friend over her boyfriend might have negative consequences on their relationship.

"It's four tickets," Mary Lou pointed out, looking amused.

"Oh... well, that would work. Only I can't really leave Auntie Clem's Bakery to go on a vacation right now." Even as she said it, Erin remembered telling Vic that once they got the new workers trained, they could take a holiday together. She pushed a tendril of hair away from her face, feeling herself flush.

"I'm sure you can find a way to work it out," Mary Lou assured her. "It will be good for you to get away from Bald Eagle Falls and all of the drama that has taken place lately."

"Right." Erin nodded, still feeling a little shocked by the news.

Mary Lou smiled and patted her arm. "At least you won't be stumbling over any bodies on an Alaskan cruise."

Did you enjoy this book?
Reviews and recommendations are vital to making a book successful. Please leave a review at your favorite book store or review site and share it with your friends.

**Don't miss the following bonus material:**

Sign up for mailing list to get a free ebook
Read a sneak preview chapter
Learn more about the author

Sign up for my mailing list at pdworkman.com and get Gluten-Free Murder for free!

JOIN MY MAILING LIST AND

# Download a sweet mystery for free

# Sneak Preview
# Vegan Baked Alaska

I*N* Erin's dream, it was dark. Pitch black. She was feeling around, trying to figure out where she was and how she had gotten there. Her stomach roiled and sweat dripped down her face and ran down her back. All she could feel around her was rock. At first, she could stand up and walk along the long passageway, but the roof kept getting lower and lower until she was crouching, and then crawling on her hands and knees, worrying about how she was going to slither along on her belly if it got any lower. How was she going to get out if the tunnel dwindled down to nothing?

How had she gotten in there in the first place? She couldn't remember, but her mind flashed back to the time that she had been hit over the head and left bound and unconscious in the endless mazes of underground caves when she had first moved to Bald Eagle Falls. Had it happened again? Or was she somehow back there? Every thought she tried to focus on slipped away from her, as they did in dreams, slithering away along the tunnel into nothingness.

# APPLE-ACHIAN TREASURE

Then it started to get lighter. At first, there was just a faint grayness that Erin barely even registered. But as she continued on, it got gradually brighter and brighter, until she could finally see the walls around her. Rather than getting lower, the ceiling started to rise, and eventually, she was able to stand again, looking around her in confusion. She was in her kitchen at the new Auntie Clem's Bakery. Was there another underground tunnel leading into the bakery? But how had it led into the bakery kitchen, which was above ground, rather than into the basement? Erin shook her head and looked around the way she had come, but was unable to identify the door she had come in.

When she turned around again, she screamed. There was Vic, her lovely bakery assistant, sprawled out on the floor, unmoving, just where Mr. Oglethorpe had lain. Her silky blond hair was spread out on the floor around her head.

"Erin! Erin, wake up!"

It was a few seconds before Erin could make the transition from the nightmare to the real world, where Terry was shaking her. She stopped screaming. Or stopped the strangled sobbing that had escaped her in the midst of the dream.

"It's okay," Officer Terry Piper soothed. "It's okay, it was just a dream, Erin."

She was shaking. Her whole body was vibrating. She melted into his arms, snuggling in close to his warm body and trying to calm herself down.

"Just a silly dream," Erin acknowledged. "It's fine. It was just a dream."

"That's right." He stroked her short, dark hair soothingly.

She breathed in the smell of his body, familiar and comforting, as she pressed her face into his chest. Terry wouldn't let anything happen to her. He wouldn't let her get hurt or kidnapped or trapped in a tunnel. All of that was in the past. Her future in Bald Eagle Falls was bright. Bright and normal, with no more murders or investigations.

"Do you want to talk about it?" Terry murmured.

"I was in a cave… and then in the kitchen, and Vic was there," Erin didn't want to put it all into words, afraid that if she said them they would somehow become more real. "She was… on the floor…"

She didn't explain any further. Terry held onto her, his grip tightening a little. He kissed the top of her head.

"Victoria is just fine. She's at home sleeping, just like you."

"She's okay," Erin repeated. The memory of Vic and her other friends being trapped in a collapsed mine was still too fresh. It was still all too familiar, that knowledge that something awful had happened to them and they might not get out alive. Erin had been swallowed up by that dread, waiting for the rescuers to drill through the rock and find out what kind of condition her friends were in. The whole time, she kept trying to block out visions of their dead bodies in her mind. Buried by rock.

Erin let out a long, shuddering breath. She turned her head to look at the clock.

"I don't know if I can go back to sleep."

Terry shifted around to look at it himself. It wasn't even light outside, but Erin was used to keeping baker's hours, and even on a day off, her body still expected to get up before dawn to start doing the day's baking. The nightmares often took place just before rising.

"Stay with me just a little longer," Terry suggested.

Erin couldn't turn him down. She nodded and snuggled back down into his embrace.

"Thank you," she told him.

"You just stay there and relax. It will all be okay. It wasn't real."

"I know. I just… it feels real. I get so freaked out."

## APPLE-ACHIAN TREASURE

"Yeah." She wondered whether any of it bothered Terry. Just because he was a police officer, that didn't mean that he too wasn't affected by the deaths and accidents that they had experienced since Erin moved to Bald Eagle Falls. Even first responders could end up with PTSD. Not that Erin had PTSD.

Terry kissed the top of her head. "When I'm not here…" he trailed off.

They didn't live together. Even if they had, Terry wouldn't be able to be there all the time, because he frequently had to take night shift or answer calls. Bald Eagle Falls had only a tiny police department, so he was often needed. He and Erin still kept separate residences, and though she did stay occasionally at Terry's, most of the time it was Terry who came over to spend the night with Erin. There was little point in doing it during the week when Erin was baking, since the hours that they would actually both be in bed at the same time were so few. So they were practical and only slept together on the nights that they could both get off, when they could actually spend time together.

"Do you have dreams when I'm not here?" Terry asked.

"Yeah… of course…" And without him there to wake her up from them, the dreams seemed to go on forever. Sometimes it seemed like she was battling her demons all night. Waking up in the morning was a relief, even if she felt like she hadn't had a good night's sleep. She just wanted the nightmares to end and to get on with life.

He gave her a little squeeze. "Have you thought any more about counseling? You've been through a lot and it could help."

"I know." Erin sighed. The last thing she wanted was more hours in a therapist's office. But she was growing more desperate to end the dreams. She had thought they would just fade away as the memory of the mine collapse and the other traumatic events that had occurred in Bald Eagle Falls grew more distant. But so far, that wasn't happening. She supposed it could take months, even years. People dealt with PTSD or other disorders for a long time. "Maybe. I really… I just don't like doctors. I've done enough of that in the past. My social workers were always insisting on different kinds of therapy or counselling. Any time I had a hard time 'settling into' a new family. It was just a… a farce. Some of them were so stupid… I knew the drill better than the professionals did. I could have given them therapy. 'Tell me about your feelings.'"

Terry chuckled. "I bet you'd make a good therapist. You're good at making people feel better."

"That'd be the carbs," Erin laughed. "Donuts really do soothe the soul."

"Well, they certainly don't hurt," Terry agreed.

Erin could hear the smile in his voice and could picture the little dimple that would appear on her Officer Handsome's face as he was speaking.

She shifted restlessly. While it would be nice to fall back asleep in his arms, she knew that it would just begin another cycle of nightmares. She didn't want to keep dreaming. Her body was more than ready to get up. She would let Terry sleep for a few more hours undisturbed.

"I'll see you later," Erin whispered. She kissed him briefly and slid out of bed, not wanting him to be so wide awake that he wouldn't be able to get back to sleep again. His normal schedule did not have him getting up so early. If he got up with her, he would be shorting himself by several hours.

"Good night," Terry murmured. "Come back and get me if you need anything."

"Shh," she told him, and she slipped quietly out of the room, shutting the door quietly so that he wouldn't be disturbed by the sounds of her moving around the house.

Orange Blossom had jumped down off the bed and was trying to squeeze through the door as Erin shut it, letting out a yowling protest when she caught his tail.

## APPLE-ACHIAN TREASURE

"Oh, Blossom!" Erin held the door ajar for a moment to make sure he was all the way through, and then pulled it shut. "You've got to be quicker if you want to get through the door before I shut it." She bent down and held her hand out for him. It was dark, but not too dark for her to see his shape in the hall as he considered whether to approach her and get his pats and ear scratches or whether to remain aloof and express to her how she had injured his pride by shutting his tail in the door the way she had.

Pats and ear scratches won out and he slid his body under her hand, turned, and returned rubbing his jowls against her fingers. He made little inquiring noises as she patted him and scratched all of his favorite places. Erin whispered to him, careful not to wake Terry any further.

"There, that's nice, isn't it? All is forgiven? I'm sorry I shut your tail in the door, but you really do need to be more careful. Maybe you should sleep in your kitty bed instead of on my bed when Terry's here."

He made a chirruping sound, as if to ask why he would want to sleep on a cat bed when he was obviously a human. Erin laughed and showered him with affection. Then she stood up.

"I need to use the commode and then let's decide what we need to do today. I'll make coffee and we'll start a list."

He allowed her to use the bathroom all by herself without pushing his way in or yowling outside the door. He was affectionate and expressive and in the early days, had frequently disturbed the neighbors with his demands for attention. But he had mellowed. Like a clingy child, he had eventually been soothed by her routines and gotten used to her comings and goings.

But he was standing right outside the door when she came out of the bathroom, nearly tripping her.

"Come on," Erin ordered. "Coffee. Kitchen."

He stared at her like he had no idea what she was talking about, but Erin knew better. He recognized a lot more words than he liked to let on, and sometimes gave away that he understood a lot more of what she said than a cat had a right to. Erin gave him a little nudge with her foot.

"Go on, don't block the doorway. We're going to the kitchen."

He allowed her to push him out of the way, but still gave no indication he understood her.

"Do I have to promise you a treat before you'll go?"

Orange Blossom took a few steps toward the kitchen and looked back to see if she was coming. Erin laughed.

"Uh-huh. I should have known. It's a good thing you don't have fingers, or I'd never be able to get you to do anything."

She followed him into the kitchen and after turning on the light, grabbed the treat can from the pantry. She picked out a few treats and sent them sliding across the floor, laughing at Orange Blossom skittering after them on the polished floor. She heard K9's almost-supersonic whine, and when Orange Blossom was finished his treat, she let Terry's furry partner out of his kennel. He waited politely for a doggie biscuit and lay down with it between his front paws as he gnawed on it. Marshmallow lolloped in on almost-silent feet, then kicked the cupboard with a hind foot to make sure she knew he was there and waiting for his treat too. Erin gave him a carrot from the fridge, which he started to gnaw on loudly.

Erin put on the coffee and sat down with a notepad to plan out her day. She was still getting used to the idea of having days off like a normal person. The extra money she had made from wild ginseng meant that she could afford to hire a couple of workers to cover the Saturday shifts and some afternoon shifts during the week so that neither she nor Vic would have to work long hours six days a week. The short Sunday shift for the ladies' tea didn't really count, since all of them, even Charley, took turns at that.

## APPLE-ACHIAN TREASURE

Erin had a hard time turning off her business owner's mind on days off. There were promotions and advertising to plan, experimenting with new gluten-free recipes for the bakery, and working out employee shifts for the coming weeks. She tried to schedule time for herself as well, reading Clementine's old journals and thick family history books and files and spending time with Terry and her friends, rather than letting her time fill up with housework and errands.

By the time the coffee was ready, she had several rough lists going. K9 had finished eating his biscuit and was lying companionably beside her, while Orange Blossom was glaring at his rival from across the room, washing his face and pouting. Marshmallow nibbled delicately on what remained on his carrot, watching Erin with one eye.

~ ~ ~

*Vegan Baked Alaska, Auntie Clem's Bakery Book 9* by P.D. Workman is available now!

# About the Author

FOR AS LONG AS P.D. Workman can remember, the blank page has held an incredible allure. After a number of false starts, she finally wrote her first complete novel at the age of twelve. It was full of fantastic ideas. It was the spring board for many stories over the next few years. Then, forty-some novels later, P.D. Workman finally decided to start publishing. Lots more are on the way!

P.D. Workman is a devout wife and a mother of one, born and raised in Alberta, Canada. She is a homeschooler and an Executive Assistant. She has a passion for art and nature, creative cooking for special diets, and running. She loves to read, to listen to audio books, and to share books out loud with her family. She is a technology geek with a love for all kinds of gadgets and tools to make her writing and work easier and more fun. In person, she is far less well-spoken than on the written page and tends to be shy and reserved with all but those closest to her.

~ ~ ~

Please visit P.D. Workman at pdworkman.com to see what else she is working on, to join her mailing list, and to link to her social networks.

~ ~ ~

If you enjoyed this book, please take the time to recommend it to other purchasers with a review or star rating and share it with your friends!

Made in the USA
Middletown, DE
15 February 2020